and other stories

some writing about sex

ISHMAEL HOUSTON-JONES

Published by:
Yonkers International Press in 2018
http://yonkersinternational.press

ISBN: 978-1-387-87498-9

Typefaces used:
Arno Pro
Arial Rounded MT

The following have been previously published:

Prologue to the End of Everything
Farm #5 (Feature and Instituting Contemporary Idea, 1990)
Caught in the Act: A Look at Contemporary Multi-Media Performance (Aperture, 1996)
Footnotes: six choreographers inscribe the page (G+B Arts, 1998)
Catalogue for the Carnegie Art Award – Nordic Painting, (2000)
Catalogue for Lost and Found – Dance, New York, HIV/AIDS, Then and Now, (Danspace Project, New York, 2016)
Writers Who Love Too Much – new narrative 1977 – 1997 (Nightboat Books, 2017)

Kim
Best Gay Erotica 2000 (Cleis Press, 2000)

Sebastian Comes for Tea
Best American Gay Fiction, volume 2 (Little Brown, 1997)

Specimen 1
Aroused, A Collection of Erotic Writing (Thunder's Mouth Press, 2001)

Specimen 2
Aroused, A Collection of Erotic Writing (Thunder's Mouth Press, 2001)

Specimen 3
Aroused, A Collection of Erotic Writing (Thunder's Mouth Press, 2001)

This collection has been a long time coming and I have been immensely helped by a group of friends and fellow artists who read, re-read and listened to these words. Among them are Joe Westmoreland, Lucy Sexton, Kyle DeCamp, Lori E Seid, Laurie Weeks, Anne Iobst, Miguel Gutierrez, Chris Cochrane, Fred Holland, Samuel Hanson, Jonathan Walker, Frederick Kaufman, Bjarne Melgaard and Yvonne Meier.

I owe much gratitude to editors along the way: Elena Alexander, Mark Russell, Karen Finley, Dona Ann McAdams, Kevin Killian and Dodie Bellamy, Judy Hussie-Taylor, Dennis Cooper, D. Travers Scott, and Brian Bouldrey. And for this collection Samuel B. Hanson, Jaime Shearn Coan and Ben Van Buren.

In loving memory of two sex rebels:
Diane Torr (1948–2017) and Duncan Gilbert / Doran George (1969–2017)

Contents

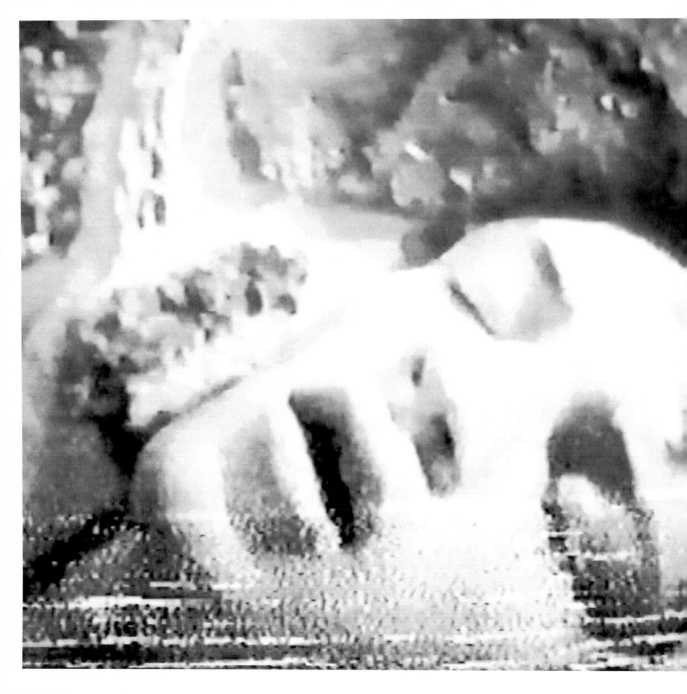

Foreword

From the unpublished *Ecstatic Obsession/Obsessive Ecstasy, The Eighties: a meditation on the films of Jean Daniel Cadinot, 1980-1990.*

My obsession with "the erotic" blossomed from my extracurricular high school reading predilections. Growing up in a conservative Northeastern state capital in the 1960s, finding sustenance to nourish my budding passion was difficult. Active in high school journalism and theater while being bombarded nightly with televised news depictions of Civil Rights abuses, the war in Viet Nam and the protests those events ignited, I became an avid reader of what was then referred to as "the underground press."

There were only two stores within walking/bicycling distance that carried these "underground" publications—the Penn Book Shoppe and Towne News.

The former was owned by an older Jewish couple with radical tastes, radical for my hometown that is. In addition to keeping an inventory of avant-garde literature, they stocked a rather extensive selection of nudie mags in the rear. I spent many Saturdays of eleventh and twelfth grade in the back of the Penn Book Shoppe.

From the back racks, under the nervous gaze of the owners, I spied worlds inhabited by hordes of naked people. Besides the smiling European "naturalists" playing summer camp sports in the nude, there were photo novellas of greasy haired hippies simulating sex in the back of shag carpeted vans. Some of these humping flower children were male and female, but the ones to which I was drawn were the ones labeled "all male."

These days, it's difficult to imagine my sixteen-year-old self with shaking sweaty hands spending hours at the back of that store. Going over and over the same publications. Never buying one, but never being told to leave either. What I did buy were paperback plays by LeRoi Jones, novels by James Baldwin, poems by Diane Di Prima and Allen Ginsberg, and political treatises by Abbie Hoffman and Eldridge Cleaver. I suppose I was such a good customer that the owners probably decided that letting this underage libertine have his time in the back of the store was his deserved bonus.

The other store, Towne News, was not run by such progressive owners. It was there that I bought my weekly *Village Voice*, which arrived about a week and a half late. I also bought my monthly *After Dark* and *Ramparts* magazines and the quarterly *Evergreen Review*. But the rule for their back section that carried "harder" products than what could be had at Penn Book Shoppe, was "No Browsing," and definitely no browsing by minors. What they did have, however, was a broad gray area between the front of the store and the back with its forbidden porn. This middle ground was stocked with detective picture magazines that featured women in black bras and black seamed stockings with garter belts, usually strangled by electric cords or stabbed multiple times. In this section were also "Muscle Magazines." There were "legitimate" ones like *Flex* or *Strength & Health*. Then there were those whose claim to be for "the serious body builder" was more dubious. One day in 1966, after months of plotting, I found the courage to buy a copy of *Flex* and a copy of *Strength & Health* with a copy of *Muscles à Go-Go* wedged in between. I still have the June 1966 edition of *Muscles à Go-Go*, with a naked blond young man wearing a transparent raincoat and twirling a clear umbrella smiling from the cover. Before my High School graduation in 1969, I had become a collector of "male erotica," with issues of *Muscles à Go-Go, Physique Pictorial* and *Tomorrow's Man* hidden in the bottom of my bottom desk drawer.

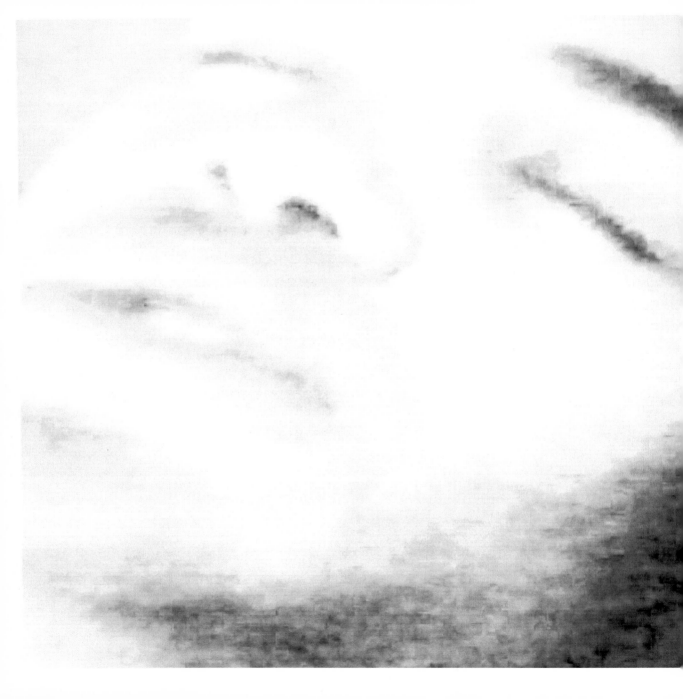

Prologue to the
End of Everything

The airport had been closed for almost two weeks; there was a ban on exit visas; Matt sleeps and dreams of iguanas calling him from a vacant lot; of strawberries the size of babies' red fists; of women in damp blouses, denim skirts and pink plastic sandals. He dreams of sucking on ice cubes. And the busboy's eyelashes.

1.   He wakes up, a wrestler defeated by his own
          sweaty sheet.

2.   He wakes up, reassured by the sounds of lizards
          on his screens and parrots in the trees.

3.   He wakes up, takes a piss in a green plastic bucket,
          takes a short look at two unhealing sores, spits out

some red foamy toothpaste, rinses his mouth with rum, takes a painful, watery, rotten-eggy shit, checks for blood, sprinkles some pine oil into the bucket…

4.   Matt heads for the cafe.
       He never liked this cafe.
       It's in the bourgie quarter across from the Palace Hotel.
       It's the only one that's still open.

5.   He steps over a few new bodies.

6.   The heat is bearable, but just.

7.   His toes curl up under, inside his boots.

8.   There are more bodies than yesterday.

9.   And a few left over from the day before.

10.   The squads are getting sloppy.
       Or overworked.

11.   He gets to the Palace.

12.   The same woman and little girl are begging on the corner.

13.   The woman is dead.

14.   The girl holds a cup. Stares straight ahead.

15.   A sign in her language is taped to her T-shirt.

16.   It reads—"Blessed Mother, protect my precious one."

17.   He drops some sweat-crumpled bills into the cup.

18.   About 25 1/2 cents U.S.

19.   The girl doesn't say thank you, not even automatically.

20.   He thinks, this is unusual, he thinks.

21.   He thinks—she'll probably be dead by nightfall.

22.   At the cafe, his favorite waitress tells him a nephew died last evening.

23.   That's four people in her family this month.

24.   He expresses his sorrow and orders a rum.

25.   He orders a rum.

26.   There's an attractive university student reading Franz Fanon at the next table.

27.   There are listless parrots in huge cages.

28.   There's the busboy he always overtips.

29.   He orders a rum.

30.   He orders a rum.
        This one with a bottle of Coke.
        With the cap still on please.
        And he adds needlessly—
        Of course without ice.

31.   He strains to see the headlines on the cute student's newspaper.

32.   Death toll, as always, in the upper right corner. And assurances that scientific help is coming from the outside. A message from the First Lady. Something about the World Futbol Cup.

33.   And a factory nearby that manufactures binary chemical weapons has been taken over by…

34.   But the attractive student's nose has begun to bleed.

35.   Badly.

36.   And people are running down the street past the Palace Hotel.

Ripping up shrubbery.
Throwing paving stones.

37.   It's a lot like TV.

38.   The waitress gives the attractive student a kitchen rag and tilts his head back.

39.   More people are running screaming in the streets.

40.   The parrots wake up to beat their wings against the bars of their cages.

41.   He hears what could be firecrackers or gunshots or mortar fire and he thinks he really should learn the difference.

42.   He thinks out loud—"What I should do is get my black ass back to New York and fast."

43.   Paving stones are being thrown at the cafe. Tables overturned.

44.   The busboy says, "Follow me, you'll be safe," and leads him into the walk-in box.

45.   All he can hear is the sound of the motor.
All he can feel is cool air.
All he can smell is fresh clean blood.

46. The busboy says in his language, "*We'll* be safe here."

47. The busboy sticks his tongue in his mouth.

48. Matt thinks of Elizabeth's latest letter asking why he doesn't come home and take that teaching job.

49. The busboy unbuttons Matt's pants, pulls them down and spins him around 180.

50. He thinks of his father teaching him to ride a two-wheeler.

51. He supports himself holding onto the cold slimy carcasses of two calves hanging from meat hooks—skinny as dogs.

52. He hears the busboy's pants unzip behind him and he thinks of paintings by Francis Bacon.

53. The busboy slaps his ass.

54. He hears a loud explosion out beyond the heavy metal door and the cool.
     More screams.
     More breaking glass.
     More parrot squawks and firecrackers.

55.   "Your legs are very beautiful but what are those marks?" asks the busboy in his language.

56.   "It's the end," Matt answers.

57.   Then, "No, it's not the end."

58.   His fingers dig into the fat and muscle of the two hanging calves.

59.   The busboy orders, "Relax!"

60.   It's not the end.
It's the beginning.
The beginning of the end of everything.

Kim

Little Friend of All the World

"I'm not good at this," I think through the graceless minutes between the exchange of cash and the nakedness. Reared by a Black Baptist mother, I want to offer him tea or a soft drink. I do offer a choice of music, although he doesn't seem too impressed by my selections.

"Hey man, this is your scene; you be in charge, O.K.?" Sure, sure. I put on a CD that I hope will be neutral enough that he won't think I'm totally pathetic. Something hip but retro with queer references but not obviously faggy. He looks bored and we've only just begun. "That the bedroom through there?" Why yes, so it is.

I see his face and I don't know what to make of it. It seems so predigested and predictable. A cliché from movies or magazines or pop songs. In reality, I am more focused on his moods and their tiny shifts within such a minuscule range. As I said, he starts off bored. More than bored. Annoyed by this apparent waste of his very precious time. I catch him sneaking glances at the clock on the VCR. Once the clothes come off, which takes about 27 seconds, he switches into something like that fake TV sitcom acting. You know, when one character is trying to keep something from another while a third, who is in on the caper, is present.

That is, he pretends to be hot for what's about to come in a way that is sure to let me know that he really is not. Too much lip licking and pouting.

"Nice bed." Yes, it is, I guess. He stretches out both bare skinny arms in a totally inauthentic gesture to welcome me into his embrace. I accept fully and fall into him; close my eyes; wait.

"There, there. Now, now." He's doing the maternal thing. Rubbing a circle on my back with a palm that barely touches me. He smells like Cuervo Gold and Marlboro Mediums. I'm still wearing my underwear. Now it's me who's eyeing the clock. Monday 11:07 P.M. Better get started.

He makes it clear that he doesn't want to be kissed on the mouth. I make it clear that I want to kiss him. It's a buyer's market as I tongue among the teeth and loose crumbs of corn chips. I bite his neck and he butts me away with his head. "Watch it. No marks, remember?" I don't remember. That is, I don't remember that being part of our contract, but, whatever. I grab his wrists with more force than I need to raise his arms above his head. He pretends to resist. I burrow my nose and mouth into one, then, the other of his sparsely haired armpits. He wriggles and quivers as I tickle him there with my tongue; as I pull and suck loose strands of pit hair. Thankfully he doesn't wear deodorant but is reasonably clean anyway. I suck on his nipples, which gets less of a reaction than I expect, so I move on down.

I continue the theme of burying my face into his other damp hairy crevices. And yes, I kiss his long bony feet and the backs of his knees. Sometimes he's with me; sometimes not. Most often he watches. From far away. I feel too active and frenetic. He has become the embodiment of stillness; almost Zen. I can jockey him around like some nude GI Joe doll. Reorganize limbs any way I want them. But like the toy soldier, his face always stays the same. It's the one thing about him that I need to change. The phrase "by any means necessary" pops into my head and I shudder at the implications—physical, sexual, political, criminal.

I had a perverted subletter earlier this year who left behind in a bag of toys, among other stuff, a bottle of poppers and a 12-pack of surgical gloves. I haven't been into amyl since the mid-70s and I've never worn hand rubbers, but right now I'm super conscious that I might be boring my naked hireling and I think, "Maybe this will entertain the little shit." I snap a glove onto my right hand and begin to glide it over his back and butt.

It's frictionless. "Hmmm, that feels good." I slap his ass, "So does that." I lift his passive little behind up from the mattress and spank him again and again and again 'til I begin to get bored and his buns have reddened. I reach for a tube of super lube that the perv left behind and bathe my gloved hand with it. I slather a liberal amount in his ass crack and still I get no reaction. So I probe with my middle finger. I'm reminded of the yearly embarrassment when during my prostate exam my young doctor nervously performs this exact act with the shy apology, "You may experience some discomfort." I always involuntarily smirk and chuckle a bit which makes Dr. Mike even more tense. Here in my own bedroom I could be poking a rolled medallion of raw veal for all the response I'm getting. I twizzle my finger around feeling the wrinkled walls of his insides. Occasionally my fingertip comes across unmoored bits of stuff. Curious. I withdraw part way, then add one, then two more fingers. His head turns quickly to look at me, then looks away. He gathers some pillows and clutches them to his chest. Is this the reaction I was waiting for? I'm not sure, but for now it will have to do. I braid and unbraid and rebraid my three fingers inside him. I hear a change in his breathing. Or is it mine? I think that I should say something so I place my ungloved left hand on the small of his back, which is now beaded with sweat. "You O.K.?"

He responds with a grunt that sounds like it could be a "yes" so I continue. I've never done this before; I'm a little apprehensive. I'm also spellbound by the act and I need to keep it going. I glance at the VCR clock and see that contractually there are 25 minutes to go. I pull back my three fingers and prepare to squeeze in the fourth. I rummage left-handed in the bag and gather five or six wooden clothespins. I slowly, meticulously decorate his dainty dick and scrotum. He silently flinches as each pin is added. Good. Good. I uncap the vial of poppers with my left hand and my teeth and place it under his nose. "Breathe in." He does and in slide my four fingers, my thumb tucked into the fold. I'm in as far as the last knuckles which surprises and scares me. I pause. He says nothing. He's breathing loudly. He's clutching those pillows as he would a flotation device after a water landing. I push the vial under his nose again, though no more forward progress seems possible. I think, "I want to feel his bleeding heart beating in my hand." Then I think, "What for?" He takes the poppers from me and inhales once, once more, then again. I've been twisting my hand around and back, around and back. He adjusts his spine, snakelike, supple. Slowly my hand is sucked in beyond its hump. His asshole is braceletting my wrist. I feel lightheaded and woozy. I'm not sure what to do now. Again I ask how he's doing. Again I get a grunt in reply.

That I'm aware that the CD has changed, that there's a drip in the kitchen and that a car alarm just went off troubles me. Those extraneous sounds should be banished from my brain by the feat of reaching up inside a man's belly and being shackled there by his anus. But no, I remember that my American Express is overdue; Mother's birthday is next month. The room smells like a giant fart. He told me his name was "Kim" which I'm sure is a lie. Clumsily, with my free hand, I reach for a disposable camera on the night stand and take a picture of him from the waist down. I wonder if I'll have the guts to get it developed at the corner Fotomat. The clock says we have eleven more minutes. I prepare to liberate myself. I smear my naked left hand up and down in the pool of sweat caught in a deep furrow of his back. Slowly, slowly, slowly. Then suddenly I'm out. He makes an even more guttural sound than before. "Are you all right?" The greasy glove is flecked with his shit. Now he's whimpering, but he hasn't moved. "Are you all right?" He rolls to his side facing away from me and chokes, "Just let me lie here and talk to myself for a minute."

I get up to dispose of the glove, smelling it first, of course. There is no blood so I feel confident that I haven't caused any permanent damage. Physically at least. There's an opened 40-ounce of Budweiser in the fridge. I take a long swig then get a roll of toilet paper that I bring back to the bed. He's still murmuring to himself, folded tightly around my pillows. I put the 40 and the TP on the mattress in front of him. He takes the bottle of beer and nurses it as if he were its baby. He won't look at me. I look at the VCR. "Uh, officially we're off the clock now, right?" He nods in my direction. I'm still in my underwear. I change the music and go to my desk and begin to write this:

...

"'I'm not good at this,' I thought through the silence in the minutes before his clothes came off. Reared by a Southern Baptist mother, I wanted to offer tea or a soft drink…"

I smoke two American Spirit Lights, make a cup of coffee, smell my pits and play some Solitaire before I finish with:

"…I changed the music and went to my desk and wrote."

...

It's been an hour and twenty minutes. I've been so wrapped up in the chronicling of the night's events that I've forgotten that there's an actual person lying in my bed. He's still cocooning around my pillows, holding the empty beer bottle. He's motionless which spooks me. I touch his shoulder. His skin is icy cool. I flash on two words—"Man/One." Then there's a slight rise and fall in his rib cage. I shake him lightly, then some more. His body mini-spasms. "Hey Kim, time to go." His head and eyes drift toward me. Hazy but alive. He unravels a winding string of words that includes questions concerning the time and whether he can stay just a little while longer. He curls away from me again, closing his eyes. I take the empty from him, "I'll get you something to drink." He shrugs his whole body. In the kitchen, I drop the bottle into my recycling box and pour him some filtered water. Back in the bedroom I sit next to him, "Here." He's snoring softly. He defines calm. Peace. I rub the cool sweaty glass between his shoulder blades. He shudders away. "Kim… Kim." Since I'm convinced that that's not his real name, it's me who's doing the bad acting now—World War II British army nurse to wounded American soldier. "Kim, you must wake up now." No, he's a giant contented baby, snoozing serenely, with big feet and a greasy butt.

It's late. I'm tired. I'm seduced by his apparent tranquility. There's dancing under his eyelids as his lips suckle mutely. I begin gathering the detritus of our debauchery. I put the vial of poppers, opened package of gloves, tube of lube back into the toy bag. Gingerly defusing a bomb, I unclip each clothespin from his puny genitalia. There is no explosion. I cover him with Aunt Bonnie's crazy quilt. I stuff an extra twenty into his sleeping fist, take one pillow away from him, a blanket from the floor and go to the sofa and crash.

…

BREAKFAST
Hey Stud,
I should've charged you extra for that little scene. I'm too nice a guy, I guess. I guess I lack certain business skills. I can't find one of my socks (not important) or my black baseball cap (muy importante). I think they might be under you but I don't want to wake you up. If (when) you find them, you know how to find me. Or I can get them when I come over next time. Hint, hint. Anyway, it was weird but hot.
Friends to the end,
Kim.

P.S. I started reading what you wrote but it was like hearing my voice on the answering machine. Maybe when you get famous you can give me a free autographed copy. Or when I marry a rich Senator you can use it to

blackmail us.
Anyway, whatever.
K.

P.P.S. Oopsie. Your door doesn't lock without a key. Hope nobody comes in and kills you in your sleep.
K.

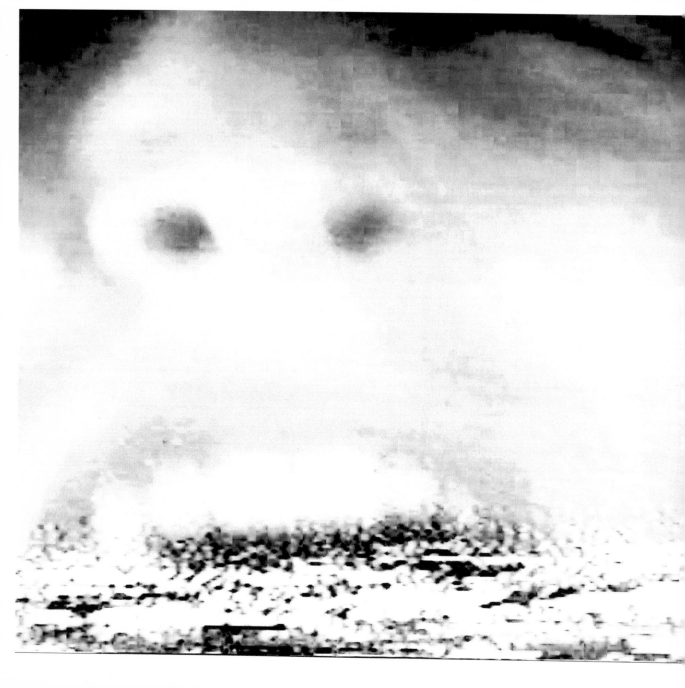

Sebastian Comes for Tea

That he lowers himself down onto me so willingly is stunning. Onto me. How strange to identify one physical part as the whole. As though the sum of my being were contained in this rubber encased, blood engorged cylinder. Anyway, what is amazing about this entombment of me by his sphincter is his previous disinclination to even consider doing it. I think this has as much to do with his fear of smell as it does with his fear of pain. Fear of smelling himself. Fear of smelling what will come out of him. Fear of proof; of evidence. He showers at least three times a day. There will be plans to meet, to go to a movie, a club, wherever, but then there will always be the delay for a shower first. I'm used to it. It's a part of him, like the color of his hair. I remember the first time I stuck my tongue "up there." How he coiled and curled and tried to get his butt away from my face. There was no pain involved then. No entrance. No "splitting open and ripping asunder." No, his discomfort was in having my nose in such daring proximity to the source of his shit. He wouldn't kiss me on the mouth for weeks after. He often remarks on the body odor of one or another of his young friends. A pungent scent is verboten. So here he is tonight, squatting, facing me, naked, greased and ready. Or at least, greased and not unwilling.

He grimaces but says nothing. What is there to say but some stale porn utterances. I can't tell what my face is doing but I can feel the muscles around the bridge of my nose going in several directions at once.

He drops another inch or so then stops suddenly and grips. Quick little intake of breath. He bares his bottom teeth then continues slowly, with not much joy in his eyes. I feel my toes contract and for a second the pain at the arch of my left foot takes me away from here. The pressure of his weight sitting full on my pelvis, my entire dick beating inside his rectum, brings me back quickly enough.

There's an awkwardness of choreography in this position. Missed cadences. Unsure balances. We're not at all like the golden boys on the video tapes. There's no mind-numbing synthesizer music washing over this scene. The lighting is just what's here—a string of colored Christmas twinklers in the next room, and from the window, orange/white street lamp, the full moon. No, the real beauty of this moment comes from the surprise of his maneuver. At once yielding and pliant while at the same time resistantly in control of the dance.

Maybe he smiles. Maybe he's just stifling a fart. At any rate he begins to rock back and forth, slowly, insistently, but when I try to arch up into him he spreads a hand down onto the space between my chest and my belly as if to say, "No, just lie still." I obey. Maybe I close my eyes.

The rhythm of his rocking accelerates. I throb inside him. The whole scene is becoming moist and messy. Yes, I begin to get faint whiffs of his insides. The rocking stops. If my eyes have been closed I open them. His hands are wet with his sperm. He makes the smallest sound possible when he comes. His face is red.

I need to end this. I grasp the front of his thighs to hold him in place. My pelvis writhes against his with regular little pulses. His hand on my chest can't stop me now. Spent, he's as flimsy as a dishrag; as weak as a feather. I drive deeper and harder up toward his core. His face looks miserable. His hair is everywhere. He, too, wants this to be over. I begin to question what it all means; him giving himself to me this way. Can't be explained away by booze or drugs or mere attraction. I wonder why, why tonight. I'm becoming distracted from the task at hand. I grip his thighs so tightly that I'm sure there will be marks tomorrow. There needs to be one part of him that I know I will find sexy. I focus on his throat and its bobbing Adam's apple. I won't tell what I imagine, but within seconds I am ejaculating inside him with some appropriate pre-language growl.

In one move, he's off me, down the hall in the bathroom with the door closed behind him. I am too drained to stop him even if I want to. After a long while I hear the toilet flush and the shower run. I peel off our condom. My room reeks of us. Bits of him and me are drying on my skin. I use some piece of his underclothing to wipe myself. I try to join him but he has locked the door. I piss into an empty juice container and crawl back into my damp, soiled and disheveled bed. When he has thoroughly cleansed himself, I hope that he will leave.

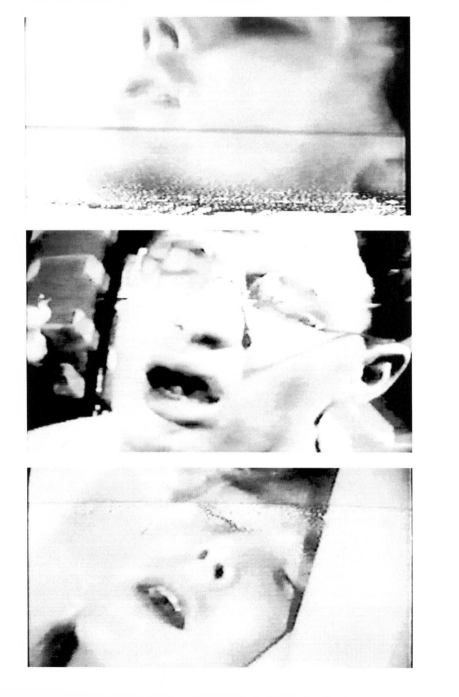

Specimen 1

FACE

The nose is crooked. Discoloration at the tip. Lips curve up. He closes his eyes.

Single earring, loop? hoop? Whatever. Perfectly formed ears. What do you call that grouping of stray hairs under the center of the lower lip? Pock marked temple. Fingers touch. Eyebrows almost taper at the ends. They scrunch together in the center of his forehead.

…

Beginnings of some kind of mustache. His feet are moving in dirty, wet socks.

…

Stud earring in the other ear.
Hair. Mostly dark brown. Looks greasy.
Crinkles brow as he looks around the room.

...

Face red. There's a smirk. Weak chin. The feminine inside of him intrigues me.
Bored. He looks bored
His eyes are tearing. No nose hair. Lips part.
Swallow.
Keep writing, Dude.
Crumpled face. Really ugly folds under the eyelids when he closes them tightly. Slight smile. Remembering? What? Egg shaped brow. Nervous flutter of eyelid. White teeth—surprising since he smokes so much. Mouthing the words of the Pet Shop Boys song on the CD player.
"Love comes quickly, whatever you do/ you can't stop falling, ooh-ooh, ooh"

...

SHIRT OFF
Redder from the neck up than the chest.
Nipples: oval—like oval quarters—that's not quite it. "Dusty Rose," darker than the chest skin—not pink.
Blue/green veins under the skin in the pits. About 20 hairs under each arm. Protrusion of ribs.

...

Back to the nose. I can't quite get it.
Nervous swallow.

...

Breathing in the belly. Weirdly small belly button. Faint hairs start in the valley of the ribs.
Mole, off to the right, mid-chest.
Moles around belly-button. Random hairs. The navel itself looks like it wasn't created by a knot. It's almost non-existent. A mere indentation. Slightly brown and then a slit. Some dark hairs- a few long ones growing from the center. Looks like an ass hole.
His pits are almost scentless. No deodorant. No soap. No sweat. Strange.

...

BACK:
Dent marks from clothes or sheets. Upper back looks almost tanned. Scattering of moles.

...

THIGHS:
Heavier than I imagined. Few scars on legs. A tiny birthmark on back of left thigh.

...

FEET:
Long. Long bony toes. Clean under the nails. Hairs on top of arch.
Well formed.
Nice legs.
God is that the best you can do? Jesus.
His legs are tanned up to the mid-thigh. He looks really bored.
Feet are cold and without smell.
Boo-boo on ankle.
[He's fiddling with his hair.]
[Where does he want to be?]
[Thinking of the $?]

. . .

IN MY BATHROOM:
He's pee-shy. He holds it underhanded—thumb over top.
He pees.
Yippee!
He's peeing a lot.

. . .

HE'S NAKED.
Drops of piss on his thigh. Penis is small and unthreatening. There's a
drop of pee hanging off the head. Pubic hair is dark brown and straight.
Ball sac is loose and red underneath. He has a rash that he thought he
had to explain. He's circumcised. A brown circle rings him mid-dick.
White spots on the scrotum.
Even his pubes smell clean.—There's almost something medicinal
about the odor.

Specimen 1

...

He's smelling his hair.

...

ON HIS BELLY.
Tiny, White-boy butt. Red blotch at the top of the crack…
Unmuscular back.
Shiny scrotum.
Right leg straight; left bent.
Birthmark mid-back on the left.
I can't get the soles of the feet.

...

O.K., THE ASSHOLE—
The buns are hairless but in the crack straight brown hairs radiate
outward. The slit is near perfect. No "roids." Pink and wrinkled. No
sign of brown.
Holding it open—there's a blue/purple vein encircling the pucker.
Remarkably—or maybe not—there's no smell.

...

Gray stretch marks over the buns.

...

Cold feet. Skin peeling off the soles.

...

Goose flesh on the buns.

...

"I want to fuck him really hard."

...

WATCHING VIDEO TAPE. "Le Desir en Ballade" by JD Cadinot
Fold under the eyes. Droopy eyes, murky-brown. Muddy. Stray hair
over forehead. Stretch marks in front of the arm pits. Is he blushing, or
just naturally red?

...

Shallow breathing through large nose.
Hands the same size as mine but look much bonier, longer.
Open pores on forehead.
Blue/green veins down the length of arms.

...

Slight smile. Somewhat immobile. Flinch.
Eyes brighten. Then darken at the sight of an enormous black cock in
the video.
His penis stays the same. As does his scrotum. No movement.
Soles of feet clasp each other in prayer.
Right arm crooked behind him around the pillow. Thumbnail worries

against pad of middle finger.
Left hand holds edge of mattress.
Breathing in belly. Slanted eyes. Moons in the fingernails. Almost a
sneer.
Penis is growing.
[Men are fucking on-screen]
Scrotum tightening.
Eyes are slitting.
Almost no movement.

. . .

[I have to pee.]

. . .

His balls glisten.
He touches his right nipple.
He looks like a handsome young girl.
He brushes his nipple with his fingernail.
He strums his flanks.
When he stands he's nearly buttless.
[I have to find a new way of saying "buttless."]

. . .

LISTENING TO "Male Multiple Orgasm, Step by Step"
AUDIO TAPE.
He's wearing my wool socks. He asked. His feet were cold.
He's smirking; so am I.

Swallow.
Highway of veins mapped across his torso. What's the exact size of his nipples?
Hands behind his head.
That nose: A bump in the middle, big pores, small hook.

. . .

Keep writing. Keep writing.
What's he thinking.
Where did he come from?
How was he spawned?
In what position did his parents fuck?
He's biting his lower lip. Holding his left hand over his head. His feet were cold.
I want to hit him.
Why doesn't he smell? Is he—what?
A vampire? Otherworldly?
Oh, this is mind-numbing.
Frown. Vertical lines at the bridge of his nose.

. . .

Keep writing—
Why is he here?
I mean, why am I paying to have him here?
Is this the only way I can have him here?
I want him; but I don't know what I mean by that.

. . .

He's following the instructions on the audio tape.
Roar, tiger, roar!

...

Keep writing.
I'm attached to his coldness. I'm always surprised by his warmth.
I can't believe he's doing this.
I can't believe I'm here.
He's got the beginnings of pecs.
Sitting: Back deeply furrowed at the spine.
Prominent Adam's' apple.
Clavicles look breakable.

...

His fingers are strolling down the path from his anus to the base of his scrotum.

...

I can't get the nipple shape and color right.

...

Gym biceps. He likes roaring. He's using his left hand. This is sooooooo....... goofy.
Yay!
I'm distracted by the tape.
I've never really looked at his body before. I think of him as skinny. I

now see that he has a very hot body. This is cool. He's going for it.

...

His collarbones jut out. My socks are hot on his feet. He has bony knees. He's touching himself. He's doing this. He's "feeling for his pleasure." He's hard. His hole is perfect. He wears the ring he bought in Thailand on the third finger of his right hand. His asshole is sucking. He's becoming splotchy red all over. The area between his anus and scrotum is becoming swollen. The hole in his erect penis is on the underside. His eyes are closed. He holds his dick with all his fingers. The head is purpling. He's rubbing his "clit."

...

Swallow.
One hand clutches his balls.
St. Paul's class of '88?
He's fisting himself tighter. He's smiling wistfully.
Swallow.
The cock head is pearlized gray.
I don't care if he comes.
I think he's closer.
I see his upper teeth.
Big Adam's apple.
Lips parted.

...

"I could strangle him."

…

That smacking sound of his greased dick being pumped.
Knees up and parted.
Is he becoming "multi-orgasmic?" He's chest breathing. His little buns
are thrusting. His hair is lank. Abs are wash boarding. Head turned to
side away from me. Eyes have been closed for a long while.
Hard swallow.
Left hand pumps. Right gropes scrotum.
I'm becoming bored. I want to turn on the TV.

…

"I want him to sit on my face."

…

I want to taste his cum.
Dot of nipple standing out, erect.
Swallow and change of breathing.

…

So to do this and not do this/ to fall/ to wallow/ pig wallow/ shit/ pig
shit/ English Peter walked barefoot through the pig shit in pen #8.

…

Left hand stroking.
Shudder.

Purple/gray head.
He has grown. He growls.
I want him but I'll never have him. $100 to watch him get off by himself.
Hmmmmmm? That's cool—(in all senses of the word.)
Is he still doing that "valley breathing?"
I want him to cum and leave so I can masturbate alone.
I want.
I want.
I don't know what I want. Rape? I don't really think so; besides I couldn't get away with it. I still carry guilt from that thing with the girl next door when I was eleven or twelve.

. . .

I wish I could masturbate in the "traditional" way—using hands instead of mattress humping. I'd whip out my cock and jerk off with him.

. . .

The tape is too much.
Too new age feely for this situation.
Turn it off.

. . .

This watching is cool—in all senses. He's working soooooo hard. Is my presence turning him off?
I wonder what my neighbors are doing? Or the guy across the street who walks around naked?
It never.......

Shit.
Don't start complaining.
Donna Summer—"She works hard for her money."
Is he doing this for me? It's after mid-night. All god's children should
be in bed—ALONE.
Am I not a child of God/dess? ← That's so Northern California.
I hope he's forgotten me.

. . .

Hooray!
He came.
Finally.
Substantial amount of fluid. Didn't shoot far.

. . .

Penis pulses by itself. A thread of semen connects it to his thigh.
Gleam of sperm on forearm.
Red eyes. Dreamy. Distant. Looking toward the ceiling.

. . .

Mopping up really well.
Red dick soft pointing up and to the left.
Eyes and mouth closed.
Clutch towel to chest.
Finger clavicle.
He's puny and non-ominous again.
Swallow.

It's so quiet. Rain outside. Occasional traffic. Not even breathing.
I want to smell his hands.

. . .

Patrician face. Or White trash. The desire to mess it up is redundant.
He's coming back. He's breathing. Eyes opening. Toes moving inside
my socks. A gesture of hand then back to the collarbone.

. . .

I have a chubby. (Later, Dude.)

. . .

His dick is becoming its former self.
On some level I want to embrace him.
On most levels I'm too far away.
I wish this were his place so I could put the money on the table and
leave.
Bony knees jut out in front of calves. Twisted legs.
I assume he wants to go now and is negotiating a graceful and profitable
exit.
I can't tell if he'll ever be a good whore. There are control issues.
I do want to fuck him someday—at least on a political theoretical level.
Shit. He's going to smoke in my apartment.
He's so cold blooded.
$.

Specimen 2

"What should I do, do you want me to strip right away?"
"No, wait, just sit down and relax on the couch."

"So, tell me about being fisted, Rickie."
"I've only done it a few times."
"How did you decide to do it?"
"Well, my ass has always been a turn on for me. It feels good having something up there."
"How many times have you tried it?"
"Twice."
"Where did you do it?"
"I saw an ad for a guy up on 125th Street who gives colonics."
"What did it feel like?"
"Nice."

"Did you trust the guy?"
"Now that's an important part of it. This guy, I didn't really trust him, and he tried to go further than I was prepared to go."
"Further?"
"Yeah. He wanted to keep going further up there, and I wanted him to stop."

He wears glasses.
He has vertical creases down his nose.
His glasses are wireless.
He has heavy, heavy eyebrows.
He wears a blue and green striped shirt. And a watch.

Speckled gray beard.

He swallows.

He has deep furrows around the mouth, a blunt nose, Semetic. The
Beard is neat
Pouffy hair.
Jeans, light brown Bass shoes.

"Could you please take your glasses off."
"Sure, I need to lay them down somewhere where I can find them."
"Are you blind without them?"
"No not blind, just very near sighted I need them to drive."

He has bushy arched eyebrows.
Crows feet.
Laugh lines.

No holes in ears.
"No, I could never take that kind of pain."
Mole in the palace of anxiety.
Expensive looking cheap watch.

Eyes—brown, kinda murky. Uneven.
His facial hair gives him that "evil Hebe" look like in the Nazi anti-Jewish propaganda cartoons.
He has a softer look.
He looks nervous and apprehensive.
He looks around my room then back to me.
He's, maybe, 50 years old.

His hair is styled into a fluffy almost Pompadour.
If he were an animal, what would he be?
Some kind of big sad dog. But wiry.
Dark red lips from under heavy 'stache.

"Go ahead and take your shirt off."

Tan skin, but sallow at the same time.
"Do you shave your chest?"
"My friend does it for me. He gets a kick out of doing it."
Stubble. Saggy breasts. Soft gut distended. Folds of belly.
No piercings anywhere. He couldn't stand the pain.
Flesh hangs over waistline.
For a minute I get chilled because I think he has no navel.
"Do you not have a navel?"
He shows it to me. It was hidden in a narrow crease of belly skin.
"You chew your nails."

Down to the nubs.
He wrings his hands; intertwines fingers.
He could be a killer.
Hands the same size as mine but thicker. Wrinkled fingers covered in fur; veiny and blunt with ragged nails.
Cut on the middle finger of the right hand.
No rings. No moons.

"You can undress now."

He does so quickly.
White, white feet.
Hard-on.
Thick thighs; shaved thighs.
Thick dick; shaved pubes, but not entirely. Halo of brown fuzz arcs around base of penis.
Mole on dick.
"Usually I get hard as a rock right away, I must be nervous."
You must be.
Thighs—blue veins and stretch marks.
Circumcised. Fat balls. Stubble.
"My friend shaves me, I don't know, he just seems to be into that."
"Do you ever shave him?"
"No. Well once I did, but I had to do it on the sly, so his wife wouldn't notice."
"Your friend is married then."
"Yeah, for many years. I think she must know. I mean she has to. He says he only stays with her for the kids. You can't break up a marriage. But he never has sex with her. He can only have sex with men."

Feet turned out. Nubby toe nails. Does he chew them too?
Lying on his stomach. Is he going to fall asleep?
Thin but mostly formless.
No back hair.
Some black moles dot his back. Three large and some smaller ones.

The crack—
light brown edges; faint butt pimples probably from shaving

He looks like a sleepy corpse

Heavy calves, white.
No buns. Face reddening. I want him out of here. Twitches. Is he gonna
fall asleep?
He rolls over.
I don't want to smell him.
The stubble on his stomach is disconcerting.
Nipples medium sized, like nickels, rosy pink.
Stubble on the underside of his dick.
Loose fat balls; mouth dumbly open; index finger moving against thigh.
"Uh, how old are you, Rickie." I kinda startle him awake.
"Forty-four." God! we're the same age.
"You don't have very many scars."
"Should I have more?"—Slight chuckle.

Well formed feet. Dick moves on its own. No nose hair. Eyes are not
aligned perfectly.

Sort of classic study of "The Male Nude" from turn of the century art
books. And I the blackamoor sit clothed beside him writing, like in

some strange kind of all-male "Olympia".
He's the anemic Odalisque rendered by Rodin.

A million Black men marched in D.C. yesterday and here I am today serving O.J. to a naked Jewish clinic administrator in the East Village. A million Black men and my Queer self not among them.

He doesn't want to look at me. He looks bored and alert at the same time. He looks around. He's sitting. He holds his ankle.
"Do you live alone?"
Bumpy mottled knees. Clean on the underside of feet. No corns or bunions.
Rolls empty glass between hands. Looks sad—wistful. I think he wants to have sex with me.
I get this goony grin whenever he catches me looking at him. He darts his eyes away. I wish I could make him into a serial killer. Or sadist.
Caved in chest.
I wish…
He startled me with a quick move to put the glass down.
He's lying down; feeling his cock; eyes closed; kneading his balls; Gently stroking the underside of the shaft. It grows. Lotions up. Prefers aloe hand lotion to K.Y..
Sliding hand-over-hand.
Tension in turned out legs.
Hand-over-hand.
Fat cock of medium length reddens. Ball sac tightens. Eyes close.
"Do you care if I do this?"
"No, it's good, keep going."
Do I care?
Tension in his thighs. I can see his belly button now.

Eyes scrunched together.

Short tight strokes, right handed. Jerk of head. Twitch of full body. Fast, it's over. Cum had yellowish tinge. No sound hardly at all.

"Do you have something I can wipe off with?"

I'm an ill-prepared host and have to scurry into the bedroom to find a cleanish towel.

He rests. More relaxed.

"What were you thinking?"

"I wasn't thinking of anything except maybe how good it felt."

Oh.

Looks like he's gonna fall asleep again.

Brown skin around scrotum. Deep navel. Still touching his cock as it shrinks.

Lonely, he looks lonely.

"I get away on weekends. I have a house in Western Massachusetts."

"No I was born in the Bronx"

His little blue bikinis are on my other chair. Blue jeans. White socks.

He fingers his balls. He fingers his cock. He rings that ledge around the head.

I can see him in his office being defensively unpleasant to co-workers.

Is he going to have another go? I think he's getting off on the scrutiny. He's "fiddling" with himself.

As he gets dressed:

"Is that it? I thought you'd ask more questions."

"Really? So what haven't I asked that you want to answer?"

Longish pause.

"Well… what turns me on?"

"Well, Rickie, what turns you on?"

"Oh, I don't know, being naked with my friend."

"Hmmm."

"Yeah. We're almost a perfect fit. It's almost too perfect. We've been seeing each other twice a week for almost six months. We're from different ethnic backgrounds. He likes to shave me, and to tie me up. He doesn't do anything once he ties me up, but he gets off on just doing it. But you know, he doesn't like any of that stuff done back to him. He doesn't like to be touched. We met over the internet too but we got together in person for the first time at the Mariotte. You know, I didn't really think he would show up. But he did and like I said it was perfect. Except for the wife. And the kids. We made an agreement not to know anything about each other but we broke that one almost right away. He called me from work one day and told me to call him that night at his home on Long Island. He invited me out there. His wife was very nice while I was there but he told me she threw a fit once I left. She must know, right? He takes me out to dinner. I've taken him to my place in Western Mass because there aren't any nosy neighbors nearby; but I'd never let him come up to White Plains. He calls me sometimes three times a day from work, and you know it's weird that he finds the time to do it because he's a high school principal."

His teeth are crooked and unevenly spaced.

"Let's see, that was an hour and half. Here you are. Good-bye, Rickie."

$

Specimen 3

He's shorter than me.
He sits facing me.
He's wearing gray shorts,
      his white tee-shirt has a square of pink with a green triangle
inside over his left breast.

Sips water.
      It's a humid gray day.
Looks down at the floor.

Hiking boots.
Clean/white socks.

He's stocky and solid.

Strong jaw.

Glass down.

Leans forward on elbows, hands gently hold themselves.

Fresh haircut.

Looks at art work.

Sparse hair on legs.

Driving music on CD player.

Looks around.

Quiet—We're being quiet.

He focuses like an animal.

Leans back on hands.

Looks out of side of eyes.

Checks out books on shelf.

Actively scopes out the place.

I'll sit next to him to get the face.

Does not look at me.

He's never been to this part of town.

Scratches his back.

Inspects a box of porn videos on the floor.

Tries to look behind me.

Largish thighs.

Ankles crossed.

Head tilted to one side.

Palms spread at either side of him, supporting him on the bed.

It's so quiet between us.
Easy quiet,
Gentle quiet,
Too quiet.

He could beat me up if he wanted to.

Smoothes his hair and gets some loose ones in his hand—he has to brush them away.

Picks up, examines and puts down blindfold.

I don't know what he just thought.

I think he's trying to see what I write.

He does not look bored.

Real active looking around but also takes time to study things, like my CDs, my books.

Is he casing the joint or just curious.

I want to sit next to him to zoom in closer on his face, but I feel shy and I have a need to maintain distance.

He tries to see into my bedroom through the French doors.

I should move in closer.

Vibrator under bed. He picks it up.

I tell him it's a present from my mother.

He flicks it on/off/on. Changes speeds.

He looks bemused.

He looks like an anthropologist.

Feels the vibrations.

Tries to interpret the situation.

Tries the vibrator on his muscular calves. His back. His upper back.

He asks if it's O.K. to use it.

I say it's fine.

It's fine.

"Do you work out every day?"

"I used to until 2-3 weeks ago—after mid-semester things got hectic; I don't get to go as much as I want."

He asks if I work out.

"Are you tense a lot?" he asks me

"Is that why your mother gave you this?"

What was that face?

He's enjoying the back massage. Now back to the calves

I'm assuming he has a short fat cock.

Now on the thigh.

I'm assuming virtually hairless except the usual spots.

Turns off the vibrator.

Am I still in the room?

Seems to be really listening to the Glenn Branca CD.

Sit close.

No holes in ears. Light stubble. Sort of like a goatee in the making.

Looks at me writing. Looks away.

I need to calm down.

Good ears.

I should stop mentioning moles. It seems everyone has them. One in the fold of his upper left eyelid.

Light acne scarring at the temple.

Pouty lower lip.

Take your time.

Heavy fold over eyes. Dark brown eyes. Clear.

Square jaw. Set. Looks determined.

Straight nose at too severe of a downward angle.

The fresh haircut shows skin at the side.

Description, description.

Loosen up dude.

He's so calm and I'm all over the place.

Maybe it's the drive of the music.

The newly cut black hair is tousled. Fringe covers his forehead.

What do I want to know from him?

He studies Architecture.

Anyway.

Smile. Talk about Houston. Blah, blah, blah.

Shirt off.

It was almost as though he'd never done it before. He was so awkward. First tugging at the tail. Then crossing his hands at the collar and pulling.

He'd told me of his birthmark in an email.

Mauve nipples. Perfect circles. Chest is large but not "cut," as they say. The birthmark is under his right tit and is large and messy.

He flexes and looks at his reflection in the blank TV screen.

Is he sucking in his tummy?

He leans back on his hands.

No hair on arms or chest.

Thick neck.

Breasts, while not saggy, not tight to the chest when he leans forward. Pointy. No gut, but not washboard either.

Not pale. Not brown. Is this what is meant by yellow?

A couple of chest zits.

A few stray hairs just below the deep navel peek above the waist band.

Drawstring shorts with "PENN" in red and blue letters on one leg.

Raises arm for me. The way he's doing it he looks like an amputee. The black hairs are wiry and a little thicker than I had imagined.

Starts untying boots. Careful about where he puts things. Undoes drawstring. Shorts and jockey's off in one jerk. Socks last. Puts each in it's boot.

Dick has a shiny raspberry head. Uncut with foreskin rolled back. A splay of black pubic hair fans up toward his navel. Sits with his short legs spread. Shaft of dick is a lot darker than the rest of him. Massages his left foot.

"BLUR" on CD. "Boys and Girls."

Just relax.

Squarish, blocky feet. Almost no sole prints.

Lies down—hand behind head.

Dark shiny scrotum.

The birthmark is a brown mottle over the right rib cage.

Crosses ankles. Cock leans to his left. One testicle keeps contracting and relaxing.

Dick is stiffening. Pointing upward. He holds it. Examines the pee-hole. Gropes balls. Fingers its shiny head. He's gentle with it. Thumbs the head in a circular motion over the ledge. Looks down at it. It's pointing directly up at him. I'm getting a little turned on. It's longer and not as thick as I thought it would be. He's rubbing his ankles together. I want to get out of the present tense.

He bends his dick to the side and presses it to his left thigh. Now he's fingering it like a recorder. No hair on the scrotum itself. Begins worrying with a strand of pre-cum. Rubs it between his thumb and forefinger.

Spreads legs. Squeezes balls. Tension in thighs.

He looks at his dick like he's never seen it before. Pats it as if it were a pet hamster.

I tell him to roll onto his stomach.

Cute butt. Hairless. Zitless. Some black hairs in the crack.

Some stretch marks at the bikini line. Buns lighter than back and legs.

Real barrel upper body.

Don't know if I can touch him. I want to see inside the crack. I don't need to. I can imagine.

The inside of the crack is darker brown…

He wiggles his ass. Flex.

Again it's too quiet.

Dents of socks around the ankles.

One dark spot at the top of the crack.

Satiny, hairless back.
He goes to the bathroom.

…

He's back.
He sits cross ankled on the bed

"Tell me about masturbating with the American flag."

[He'd emailed me he'd done that as the response to my question—
"What's the most deviant sexual act you'll admit to?"]

"Oh my God. I guess it was like third or fourth grade. I, um, (giggle).
It was definitely a turning point in my history of masturbation.
I first discovered the good feeling in the playground trying to climb
the pole of the jungle gym. After several attempts I noticed that it felt
really good.
After that I'd pretend to climb that pole every recess."

"Then by complete accident I was left all alone in a classroom and I
wanted to take stuff. There were two flags—one California, one U.S.
So at that young age I stole state property. I had to hide it at home."

"I noticed the feel of the fabric. I happened to be naked and started to
rub myself with it. I was just at the age when I began to be able to shoot
fluid."

"I hid it under my mattress. After eight or nine months it started to get
stained. There was a hard crust. It was like it wasn't the same material. It
felt more like plastic. It had lost its original silkiness. It was like crystal
paper. It even changed colors. I threw it out."

"The thing is, my mom's an immigrant and she always told me to revere the American flag; that if you ever let it touch the ground you should then burn it. I remember that I had no concept that what I was doing was wrong. What was funny, I never let that flag touch the carpet in my room."

Chat, chat, chat.

He tells me he's had bondage fantasies since he was a little kid. Ever since he saw Charlton Heston in *Planet of the Apes*, he wanted to be Charlton Heston being chased by the Ape-men. I try to imagine Mr. Heston as a short little Chinese kid with a cum stained American flag under his bed.

Chat, chat, chat.

His balls still periodically contract.

"I acted out these fantasies once. I got tied up with a fuck buddy. I went with some guy and got some rope but then he says, 'Lick my boots.' And I said, 'No way, I'm not going to do that'."

Chat, chat some more.

"Is it O.K. that I didn't jerk off?"

"It's fine."

It's fine.

$

Specimen 4

7 Sept 2001

It's been a long time since I've done this. This. Asked a man to come with me so that I can observe and write about him. I met this one in a club, Stella's, in mid-town. He dances there. For tips. For money. It's his job. One of them. What I know, or what I think I know. He lives in the Bronx. He's in his mid-twenties. Until this summer's heat wave he had long dreadlocks. Now his head is shaven. He sells weed. He sometimes does construction. He'd told me that for private shows he charges $100 for dancing, $250 for jerking off. I know that I don't know his real name. And that I think he's very attractive.

I call him on his cell phone. His phone voice is quite different from his voice at the club. On the phone he's tougher, more "Black," less friendly. Is it that I can't see the killer smile over the phone and I now hear the real attitude? Or maybe he just doesn't like talking over the phone. Anyway,

I call him from my office. He says he just put some things in the dryer and he'll call back in an hour. An hour and a half later I call his cell.

"What's up Playah, I was just fixin' to call you."

I tell him again where my office is and how to get into the building. He says it'll be at least an hour to get down from the Bronx. We've not discussed why he's coming down to meet me. There must be some assumptions but they've not been voiced.

More than another hour passes. I get a call. He's on the corner. I tell him I'll be right down.

We do that macho dude embrace on the street thing. One arm each, pats on the back. I've decided this interview is going to take place at the West Side Club—my home is too chaotic for visitors, even paid visitors.

The West Side Club is a gay male sex club in Chelsea. I used to go there with Specimen One after I got to know him better. I've never been there alone, un-chaperoned. I recently renewed my membership even though I hadn't been there in over two years. I'm not quite sure why I chose this as the location for the Specimen Four interview. There must be some assumptions but they've not been voiced.

It's now rush hour. There are no free taxis on Fifth Avenue. As we walk down toward Chelsea, I keep nervously looking over my shoulder to see if we can get one. We stop in a pizza place so he can buy something to drink. He asks if I want anything. He first asked for a Mountain Dew but changed his mind and got a Dr. Pepper. We continue walking down the avenue, me still looking over my shoulder, apologizing, it's driving me crazy.

He hasn't asked where we're going. I had asked that he bring a picture I.D. and that we were going to some club, I may have said some gay club, but beyond that no explanations were asked for or given.

As I said, it's been more than two years since I've come here. It's just after the evening rush on a Friday. The prices are a little higher than when I was last here. For four hours the prices are $8 for a locker, $12 for a changing room, and $16 for a room. Plus all prices are $2 more on weekends. He's going to have to get a temporary membership so that he can get a locker that he won't use. There are already guys queuing to get in. He's on guard and suspicious. He cops an attitude with the clerk in the office that I've never seen him use. More defensive and thuggish. Overall he's acting more "street" than he does when he's dancing at the club. I'm not sure if I like this change but I'm certainly intrigued by it. We get out of line, go into the office where the clerk is being concierge-like efficient, then we get back into line to get our keys; mine for a room, his for the locker he'll not use. I pay for everything.

An attendant shows us to my room. I tell him we won't need the locker He gives us two white towels and I tip him a dollar. On the way we passed guys wrapped in white towels. The man in the room next to mine is lying face down and naked on his cot. All the "rooms" are tiny. Maybe 5 by 8 feet but I'm a bad judge of dimensions. The cot is about 6 feet long and 4 feet wide and it takes up more than half the space. It's covered with a slab of foam and a sheet. There's a small nightstand and a wall mounted lamp with a dimmer switch. The walls do not go all the way to the ceiling so that there is no sound privacy. Techno music plays on the sound system. The walls are chocolate brown. There is a lot of ductwork

in the ceiling. I fiddle with the dimmer switch trying to create the right atmosphere, not too dark and sexy but definitely not too bright. I get my new notebook and pen I bought today at the stationary store. I sit on the nightstand; he sits on the bed. I begin babbling about my writing project telling him that I've had some profiles and stories published.
He just asked what "published" meant.
His hair is peach fuzzing back in.
Nicks of baldness.
Dark button eyes.
Head bobbing to music.
Long black lashes.
Narrow head.
Didn't shave.
Smiles when I tell him I'm writing about him.
Long blue short sleeve T-shirt.
Jeans.
Timberlands.
Holds onto his cell phone and fingers the antenna.
Goatee.
Smallish ears.
Dark around the eyes. (Sexy.)

"What is this place?"

His shirt is "Sean Jean."

"That's my label. That's what I like."

His birthday is November 18, (Scorpio. Of course!)
He's 24.

Born in Philly.
Doesn't remember when he came to NYC. He was a baby, **"like 2."**

How'd you start working at Stella's?

He's wearing white socks.

"Started off dancing at the Magic Touch in Queens. It's closed down now."

I thought I remembered him telling me it was a straight club.

"No it was gay."

How'd you wind up working a gay club?

"I was broke. Didn't have no money. All my other hustles not working. I said fuck it."

He went to school in the Bronx. Got his GED in Harlem.

When I took my friend Keith to Stella's he immediately noticed my attraction to this dancer. He pegged him as my type, saying that he reminded Keith of the lead singer from the group Arrested Development. Keith said, "Obviously he's had some college."

So you dropped out of high school then?

"I dropped out after the first four months of high school, took the GED the third quarter, I was fresh 16."

Tilts head back against wall while remembering.

How long were you at the Magic Touch?

"A good year, year and a half, off and on."

How did it compare to Stella's?

"Way better. Magic Touch catered more to the dancers. And the customers knew that that was a place to go see dancers. It was more dance orientated. At Stella's there's always a string attached. Money was a whole lot better. They had contests there: Dance Contests, Big Dick Contests, Butt Contests. It's like if the dancers had a complaint the managers listened. Stella's is not for your amateur dancers. They come into the game and they see the other dancers making money and 9 out of 10 times they thinking I'll start getting my dick sucked. Ain't no place for relationship, friendship with a he or she. A rookie sees that and he thinks he gotta be doing something, he thinking that's what we do. I tell somebody when I need help; not every customer's an asshole. The rookies don't see that. $50—they go get their dick sucked. I'm here to give people exotic pleasure, within my limits. I do 'live porn,' with girls. It's all about this; this is an exotic entertainment business. You're here to dance or masturbate, that's what I do. Yeah, I'm selling—somewhat hardcore, but with a little taste and class."

Smiles.
 So what do you see yourself doing five years from now?

"Just hope I'm alive. I'm not trying to be no psychic. In my lifestyle

I have to take it one day at a time. Tryin' to enjoy my young 20s, my quote/unquote 'college years.' I'm tryin' to build a foundation. Hopefully five years from now I'll be buyin' a car, a house. I would like to see myself take it to the next level. Put my shit on the web. I do music. Make some movies of myself. Market myself that way."

What kind of music?

"Crazy music. A little bit of everything. I just hear something that motivates me. If people want to see me, then why wouldn't they want to hear me? Maybe tour on the East Coast."

You told me before that you're straight. Could you talk about how it feels to be touched and felt up dancing in a gay club?

"The first six months was like ... I don't know how I handled it. But then you know it's all part of the business I'm in. The exotic business. I keep my opinions in my back pocket 'cause they don't matter. I can't say 'I don't like what he do.' I let him touch me and I'm getting money out of it."

When did you decide to get into this business?

"It was always in me. When I read my first porno I always understood I'd get into this. Even when I was little. Like, why the fuck would you want to watch TV when you could have sex." (I cringe at that.) "I've always done a lot of crazy stuff. That shit just happens."
He's figuring out the architecture of the place. The space is a maze of corridors with doors on both sides. It's dim; the walls are dark. From our "room" we can see a tangle of heating ducts at the ceiling.

Guys having sex in the next "room."
His head is tilted back.

Where do you live?

"With my stepfamily. My stepfather. Stepbrother. Everybody."

Fingers his goatee.

Where did "your name" come from?

**"From PeeWee from Porky's. Everybody always said 'you actin'
like that dude PeeWee.' That just got shortened. Then I had my rap
attitude. The second part came about 'cause I was smokin' a lot of
weed. I just threw them together. It stuck. But a lot of people think
I'm called Peter. They hear Pee, but they think they hear Peter.
Whatever, it's all good. Forget about it, don't forget about it."**

He has my "room" key on its rubber band around his wrist.

Are you going to grow your dreads back?

**"Don't know. I regret cuttin' them, but it doesn't fuck with me.
It's just a frame to use, like 'My Name,' he's the guy with dreads.
Sometimes I wish I could go back in time."**

One Friday night last winter/spring I went up to Stella's. I noticed that
a lot of the regular dancers weren't there. After "Sex Appeal's" number I
asked if "P" was dancing and "Sex" told me that all the Latin boys were
dancing at Poppycock. This was the first time I got wind that there was

a distinction between the Black and Latin dancers. I quickly finished my beer and ran upstairs. I got one of the gay rags to find out where this Poppycock was, but I didn't have my reading glasses and in the dim light of the bar I couldn't read the small print of the listings. I asked a young hustler if he knew where Poppycock was but he said "no" and moved suspiciously away from me. I was desperate. I spotted "Freddie" the coat check man who is about my age and was wearing his reading glasses pushed up onto his head. I asked to borrow them. I tried to look up Poppycock but was having no luck. He asked what I was looking for and I told him. He said, "Oh that's at Speed." By this time I didn't mind looking like a loser so I asked where that was. His reply was, "Oh that's over on 39th behind the Lord and Taylor's." I grabbed my coat, left a tip and ran the whole way from 47th to 39th.

When I got to Speed, a club I'd never heard of, I got into a line of people all younger than me. When I got to the young woman who was tending the door she looked me up and down and asked which party I was there for. I told her Poppycock. She said kind of dismissively, "That's that line over there." I got into the "gay" line; funny I hadn't noticed the difference, paid too much money and entered the 3 level club that was totally unknown to me. At one point I saw "James" another dancer from Stella's and his first words to me were, "'P' was here but they sent him home." I sort of blushed that it was that obvious why I'd shown up. "James" took me up to the 3rd floor where the VIP lounge was. I was then left to figure out how this place worked on my own. There was a line forming for what I figured out was a back room. I saw people giving someone money to get inside. I asked the person ahead of me how much and he told me $5. Once inside black theatrical curtains defined a very dimly lit room. There were couches and chairs. "We" sat around and waited. The "dancers" began to filter in dressed (or rather undressed) in skimpy underwear. They performed that male version of lap dances, more explicit than at Stella's. In addition to "James," "Carlos," "Luis," and "Danny" were there. It suddenly dawned on me that the name of the place was Papi Cock not Poppycock. When each approached me they each gave me a version of why "P" wasn't there. I hadn't thought that my attraction had been that obvious. I wound up having a fun time. It was the first time I felt I connected to "James" in a direct way. Bought him some Bacardis while he danced on the bar downstairs. He gave me a verbal description of what his "private show" would be like for me. I counted at most five people in this packed club who were my age or older. I wanted to dance but felt too self-conscious to do so alone so I left, losing my scarf in the crowded cloakroom.

What happened at Papi Cock?

"Didn't like the way it was organized." Those VIP rooms is funny. Certain dancers fuck it up. You gotta be able to handle that. You can make more money there. But you think, I be hoin' and you fuck up your game."

(Couple going at it in the next room. I feel the thud of their bodies against the flimsy wall. Moans. "P" gets lost in the music.)

Where's your real family?

"In the Bronx. My mother, my sister, we're not too tight. We have a funny relationship. When I'm there we fight. When we're apart, we love each other."

If you weren't in this business what would you be doing?

"That's a fuckin' good question. Sellin' drugs, probably. What else can I do? When push comes to shove probably have a 9-to-5 and be slingin' drugs on the side. I don't like to depend on just one source of income. I'll always be doing the illegal, 'cause, why wouldn't I. I got good street credibility. I'm not stupid. Not gonna take stuff I don't need."

I've become self-conscious that the guys in the adjoining rooms can hear us talking. You're not really supposed to talk here.

He lies down on the cot. Looks up at the ductwork in the ceiling. Hands behind his head. I've been sitting on the little Formica nightstand. We're in the classic shrink/patient positions. Smack of blowjob from the next room. He looks more "knowing" than he does in the club. Small perfect nose. Not thick lips. Raspberry. Mocha skin.
Not giving anything up.
His shoes are loosely untied.
Moans and smacks coming from the rooms on either side. We're in a gay sex sandwich.

Do you want to ask me anything?

"I don't know…"
(We're quiet for a very long time.)

The weekend before this interview there had been a bachelorette party at Stella's of about 8–10 young women. The bride wore a veil. They sat at the stage-side table and were quite boisterous. The dancer "Dark Side" started doing a number just for them, carrying the bride up onto the stage and humping and spanking her to the delight of her friends but to the consternation of Bruce, the bouncer. After his number Bruce told him to leave.

I break the silence
—has "Dark Side" been 86ed forever?
Shrugs.
"See that's what I mean. They don't cater to the dancers there. They act like it's a vice versa thing but it's not. They not looking out for you."

What's up with Bruce?

"He keeps an eye out for Cathy."

Cathy is the owner of Stella's. A butch bottle blond who likes to hang outside patrol car windows and chat up the local cops.

And Cathy?

"She only comes downstairs when there's a problem. If you see her coming down the stairs, somebody's gonna get thrown out."

"People in my neighborhood crack jokes about what I do. They say I'm gonna turn gay. But I love bein' with the females. I dance for men and women. I would dance for women more but I need to dance for the men for the money. There's not enough money from the females. What I get from the females is pussy. For real. But I can get pussy on my own time. Some dancers trade dances for pussy but then they ain't talkin' about digits. If I wanted to make a lot of money I would only dance for fat girls. Yeah send me to a fat

3

farm." **Laughs.**

**"But I try to tell some of these dancers, 'where's your sense of
the game?' Me, Carlos and James are different. We know this is a
business and this is what we need to do. It's about the digits. Not
about gettin' pussy."**

**What's the most you've gotten dancing in one night? What's
normal?**

"Once I got $600, no $800."

I'm not sure he's not making these figures up.

"$200 is pushing it. Usually around $100—150."
**"You gotta please your customer, then just move on. Buy him
a drink whatever. They appreciate. They tip. That shit adds up.
Some of the other dancers see that and they start talkin' shit but
the Motha fuckaz don't understand, when females come to the club
they ain't givin' you nothin'. Now, I ain't no gay man's superhero
but get real. This is who comes to see you week in and week out.
These females come one night for a party and the dancers get all up
in them and then the girls don't tip. And the fellaz don't tip either
'cause they get pissed."**

The sound of spanking comes from another room.

"It's all good though."
He belches.
I finish his Dr. Pepper as we get ready to leave. We're both still dressed

as we make our way through the towel clad men. I think how ironic that of all the times I've done this, this time I interview someone who is actually in the business and nothing sexual happened.

Specimen 4a

11 October 2001

We meet again. Baseball cap backwards, plain white T-shirt, baggie
black sweats with side patch pocket,
Timberlands with white socks.

Nails lacquered—**"I was due."**

Hair is growing back.

It's hot in here; I'm sweating.

He has killer eyes, a goatee. He didn't shave. Hole in his ear. Eyebrows
well formed.
Long, long lashes.

We both sit on the cot. That is, I move from the nightstand to the cot. His fingertips rest on his thighs.

Take your hat off.

I feel as though I should have said "please."

His hair is very black and straight at the root. It's about 1/8 of an inch long.

I can't take it when he looks directly at me.

Rubs his hair.

Cap is a "Phillies" cap ("P").

Looks at a lube packet.

Thin raspberry lips.

His hairline recedes just a bit on each side, with a peak in the middle.

Narrow face. A few scars on his forehead.

He could be from anywhere—Middle East, Spain, Arab, Jew.

Sometimes he looks scared or intimidated. I'm calming down.

Plays with lube packet.
Puts it down.

I tell him I just wrote that.
He smiles.
I melt.

"Pass me my jacket."

I do.
He gets baggie of weed and starts breaking buds on the trashcan he's turned upside-down.

He takes off his shirt.
—**"It's extremely hot in this Motha Fucka."**

"JAH" tattooed on his left biceps. "America's Most Blunted" on his right.

Pointy nipples, just a little darker than chest skin.

He separates weed into lines.

Begins to roll.

I think—I don't want to get kicked out of here for drugs. I don't want to ask him to stop.
I don't know what will happen.

He's made a joint. I'm sweating.

I say,
I've never been here in the afternoon before.

His body. Not cut. But built. Very little body hair. Some stragglers below the navel.

He focuses on rolling the second joint.

Do you shave your body?

"Yeah, well, not my body, just my (pause) **genitalia."**

Why?

"I don't know, I don't know. For sex reasons I guess. It eliminates odor."

But not your underarms?

"No. I need to. I sure smell down there."

We're not smoking the joints; he puts them aside on the cot.

Calm again.

Listening to the jangle of keys all around us.

Trance music.

Veiny forearms.

Have you ever been arrested?

**"I got called in on a warrant. First one was for selling weed. It went
to trial. I skipped out. When I got caught for selling bootleg movies
I got caught on the old warrant. Then I was arrested for smoking
weed. I did 48 hours."**

Where?
*By which I meant where did he do the 48 hours but he answers where he
was arrested.*
"Clinton High School. Fordham Road. Over Park."

What am I doing here? I think to myself.

I sit closer.

Almost on the joints. Sorry, I think of Woody Allen blowing the cocaine
in *Annie Hall.*

Sorry.
"Don't worry about it."

Do you work out?
"Not in two months. I need to get back on it. Keep my shit together."

Where?
"A gym on Fordham Road."

Who are the girls you work with? (In your live porno shows.)
"Nobody special—just girls I meet in the clubs."

So, tell me about these live porno acts.

"Just what I tell the customer. Instead of watching a tape he can watch us live. They get to jerk off. Or direct. Like, 'do it like this. Do it like that.' Plus they get to touch me. I figure that if they payin' they might as well get to touch me."

Who are these customers?
"Regular guys. Businessmen, bankers, lawyers, one guy owns a vineyard out in California."

Where do you do the shows?
"Their place or their motel, hotel, whatever."

Do you run ads?
"No ads. I find them in the clubs. They ax me if I do private shows and I give them the rundown."

Can you take your pants off?

He does. He's not wearing underwear. I'm surprised. I wasn't quite ready for that.

He puts his Timberlands back on.

He becomes aware of the music.
I guess as it gets later the music gets more intense.

"What is this a health spa?"
I make an obscene gesture with my middle finger and the other hand as a way of explaining.

His pubes are just growing back in.
"I'm normally bald."

I tell him the only time I've ever "shaved" was when I had crabs. I'm not sure how I feel about this pube shaving thing.

He's circumcised, about five inches. He displays his big balls in his hand for me like they were some rare jewels. His dick moves on its own. The shaft is darker than the head.

Smallish hands. I think of the Hebrew word for eggs—"BAYT-tseem"—which is used for balls. Much more appropriate than "balls" or "nuts."

Have you ever done a show with another guy?
"Just dancing, that's about it."

Not hairy legs. Skinny calves. I can't believe …

What's the wildest thing you've ever done? Professionally?
"I don't know. Fuck a guy's girlfriend while he watched. I spit and pissed on some dude one time. He asked me. But I'd just smoked a blunt so I had no spit. One good lugie was it. Once a guy showed up with ropes and shit; had me nervous. But he just wanted me to tie him up and interrogate him."

I tell him I have a friend who worked as a Dom. He smiles. I am dying.

His dick keeps moving without growing. He keeps stroking the short hair on his head. Looking up at the ceiling.
I watch him breathe.

His right hand is over his left breast.

Beautiful cock.

How long were you in Puerto Rico?
"Maybe two years—6th grade and 7th grade."

A few hairs around the nipples. Deep navel. Straight black pubes.

(Pause)

He plays his ribcage in time to the music.

Could you roll over?

Looks dreamy and far away.

Almost no tan line.

"Didn't go to the beach at all this summer. Just one day, the day of
the parade. Ain't been to a tanning salon in a while either."

Cute butt, no bubble.

His left (shod) foot crosses his right leg as he lies on his belly. He plays
with end of a towel. His calves are hairy. I'm too shy to ask to see his
crack.

You used to wear an earring?
"Used to. Took that shit off a long time ago."

Small birthmark on upper thigh.

He is the most beautiful boy in the world, I smirk to myself.

The music has been off for a while.

Sounds of bare footsteps and keys jangling in the hallway beyond the door.

Quiet.

We're quiet.

I don't want to talk while the music's off. I'm curious about his feet.

Someone's cell phone rings in another room.

No overt sex sounds.

He fingers the towel.

Hasn't looked at me for a long time.

Little movement in the hips.

Yay! The music's back on.

He's bobbing his head to the rhythm.
So you've never placed an ad in the gay magazines?
"No ads. I sell weed and ecstasy and do private shows."

I thought you said you didn't do ecstasy?
"I don't do it, I just sell it."

I stand to get a better overview.

He hasn't changed position in five minutes.

Carly Simon/Janet Jackson remix of "You're So Vain."

You can roll over if you want to?

He does so right away.

Shiny scrotum.

Smiles.

This is perhaps the most masochistic thing I've ever done.

Over the loud speaker—"Room 242, please come out to the main desk." That's not us.

Do you want to jerk off?
"If you want."

He puts a towel over the entire front of his body like a tablecloth.

"Pass me one of those shits," meaning a packet of lube.

You're right handed?

He strokes out away from his body. Dick's about five. Now he's pumping back and forth. He holds the packet in his left hand. Slow to get hard. He watches his hand and cock. I keep watching his face. He has a bit of a scowl. Perfect nose. I'm hard—and fully dressed. He pumps faster. He lets go of his dick. Spurts. Not too much. Not too far. A tablespoon's worth maybe. He wipes his hands on the towel. He never looks at me. He wipes his dick really well. Squeezes out the last drop.

"I love this song."

I ask who it is. He tells me Blue Cantrell. He sees I've written B-L-U-E.

"No, it's just B-L-U."

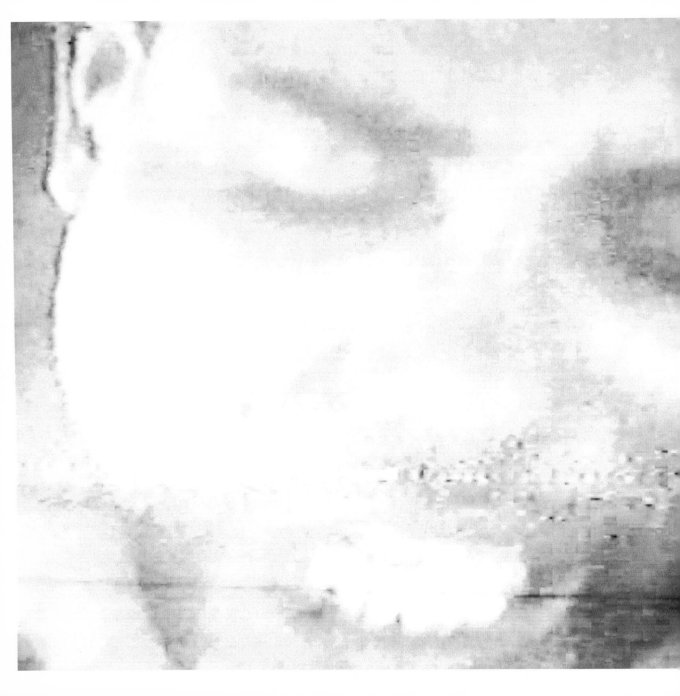

Fat

"…Two lovers entwined pass me by
And heaven knows I'm miserable now…"
—The Smiths

Saturday, 28 August 1999, East Village, New York City

Streaks of grime on glass filtered sunshine into a manageable gray. The sun had been cooking the air for hours; it glared oppressively bright beyond his dirty windows. The air, his mattress, and his fat body were all moist. "Damp" and "dank." He considered the shades of difference between the meanings of those two words. He felt that together they almost perfectly defined the present condition of his bed and himself. He could not feel the border—where his bed ended and he began. Together they were a damp, dank unit. They smelled like old onions and stale hair. Stagnant sweat. Dead skin cells flaked and rotting. The poop of dust mites. His mass and mattress shifted against one another. It would take something seismic to separate them.

He got up to pee.

He looked at his desk. He went back to bed. The doorbell rang. He held his breath and willed whoever was there to go away. The phone rang. He didn't answer it. It rang again. He got up and stood over it and listened to the answering machine as his mother left a message. He went back to bed. O.K., O.K., he bargained with himself. He could stay in bed exactly 30 minutes more if he promised to do something useful. Like masturbate. Should've been no problem. He thought. Hmmm. No. No. Shit no, no one came to mind. Done him, done them. Hmmm. Nada. He realized that at some point, he couldn't remember when, he had eliminated himself from his own masturbation fantasies. Yet it wasn't like watching porn where he could imagine spying on other people, through curtains or Venetian blinds, or peepholes. It wasn't like he'd be sitting invisible on their bed, floor, kitchen table, wherever, watching them up close and taking notes. It had come to the point now that he wasn't even there. Less than there. Not even as though he were looking through the eyes of a photo on the wall. Now he was an odor in the room. He was the air that hovered full of heavy metals and toxins near the ceiling. He looked down and what he saw could barely sustain his interest. He tried to remember some fer'instances that would get him going but he couldn't really. Porn stars, Junior High School gym teacher, someone on the subway yesterday. None of them were doing it for him.

How had getting himself off become so complicated? He recalled that in that seminal 1960s gay play (later a gay movie) one character, the self-described "pock-marked Jew fairy," extols the benefit of masturbation as never having to look your best. But then he remembered that once back in the mid-80s self-love had almost landed him in the hospital.

Even though personally he'd never been a genuine fan of

experiencing anal sex, he decided some years ago that he wanted to "explore taking it like a man." "This way I'll have one more option when not having sex with other human beings," he'd smirked. He figured a little home priming would be helpful, but he'd always found dildos to be aesthetically unpleasing; something about the pink fake flesh color or the unnaturalness of the basic black. And they always seemed so big for a semi-virgin like himself. Of course the real reason that he'd resisted using a dildo is he knew he'd be too embarrassed to go into a sex shop and buy one. But being determined to expand his sexual repertoire he decided to utilize the local 24-hour Korean vegetable stand. Late one evening he stood there taking an exceptionally long time searching for the perfect zucchini, cucumber or thin Japanese eggplant. Why didn't the colors of those vegetables bother his refined sense of aesthetics? Don't know. While he was making his choice a middle-aged house frau appeared next to him picking out her produce. Thank god for his light-brown-skin complexion so she didn't notice him blushing. He finally selected a medium sized under-ripe cucumber, the kind with lots of little bumps. He was trembling when he took it, along with his other groceries, up to the register, as though the Korean lady would immediately know and care about exactly what he was planning.

At home he'd undressed and popped in a porn video that had a lot of anal action ("Sex Bazaar" by Jean-Daniel Cadinot he recalled). Using the electric vibrating back massager with heat and extendable handle his mother had given him one Christmas he stimulated his perineum. Now maybe because it was a gift from his Mom, he'd never been able to use this device in any sexual way before. But now he was determined. He greased up the cuke and started sliding it in, watching the porn, trying to stay hard. He rolled over and "mattress humped." He came. But, "Oops!" the gherkin slipped the whole way in.

He freaked out. He got up and began pacing around his tiny apartment, bumping into things. He was fat, naked, hunched over, in a panic and trying to decide between the Beth Israel, Bellevue or St. Vincent's emergency rooms. He was trying to compose a plausible explanation when he thought he should give a try at removing the offending vegetable himself. So, oh, you should already know, once about fifteen years ago, he read a very long article in a free holistic health magazine about coffee enemas and colon care that described squatting as the most beneficial position for defecating in preventing colon cancer. Ever since then, he'd grasp the sink and clutch the windowsill in his bathroom, hop up and squat on the rim of his toilet. Now for some reason he had placed the cucumber in a condom before greasing and inserting. Maybe as a prophylactic against some plant disease. Maybe he was planning on using it in a salad later. Anyway, in the squat position, he was able to get a hold of the tail of the condom. He used the deep breathing relaxation exercise he knew and tugged gently being extra careful not to tear the rubber. After a very, very long minute "the thing" slid out. He was spared getting dressed, walking down five flights, and taking a bumpy cab ride with "that" up his butt. Not to mention doing an intake interview with some unsympathetic Emergency Room receptionist.

That memory did little to put him in the mood. He tried again. Lying there, he began to think about how memory really works. He thought "apple." The thing, not the word. If he closed his eyes he could see the object. Round—red, green or golden. He immediately saw a Granny Smith because that was his favorite. But he could change that to other types. That was to say he could remember what stuff looked like. Dead Dad in his coffin, postcard from Ruby Falls Tennessee, newborn piglets, Johnny Hardon, Coach Deibler, some boy on the subway yesterday.

But if he tried to remember the smell of the Granny Smith he'd be stumped. He tried. He knew if someone were wearing a trendy fragrance called Sour Apple, he'd recognize it immediately. But trying to conjure up the exact aroma of anything that didn't smell like snot or phlegm and it was useless. No hyacinth; no rotting fish; no banana pancake. No strawberry/herbal shampoo; no armpit. No pissy pubic hair; no butt hole. Nothing. Not even feet. So, he came to the uninspired conclusion: remembering what sex looks like is different from sex itself.

Taste is so combined with smell that anything that was not mucous, not coffee, not tobacco, not remnants of the last thing he'd eaten was pretty much moot.

But what about sound? Key in lock, yes. Bed squeak, yes. Opening riff of Marvin Gaye's "Sexual Healing," yes. Actor in bisexual porn video imitating Robert DeNiro in *Taxi Driver* while fucking a man while being ordered about by two dominatrixes who are having sex with one another, yes. Someone, unnamed, saying, "Oh, fuck me fat man," yes. Yes, he could remember the sounds of sex.

Touch was tricky. He couldn't be sure but he thought he could remember the exact satin-like oiliness of the dancer's skin, the precise feeling the first time someone touched his eleven-year-old hard-on, belt against his 13-year-old butt, whip against his 40-something-year-old back. Hmm, Master Lee. His business card was probably still buried somewhere beneath the detritus on his desk.

He'd met Master Lee during that ill-advised period when he felt that erotic "experimentation" could possibly lead to some form of contentment. "I joined the sexual revolution and all it got me was a vegetable lodged in my rectum," he sniffed. That private humiliation made him decide that Fat Solitary Jerk Off might be the banner he was fated to waddle beneath in any future Gay Pride parades.

He'd seen an announcement in a free gay bar weekly for an exhibition of S&M Tools and Techniques. He'd never been into this sub-genre of the life but since the Leather guys he'd seen around town seemed to be scarcely concerned with waist size and hair, he thought he should give them a try. He showed up early at the community center expecting a sexy dark atmosphere of screams and desire. What he found looked like an all-male P.T.A. meeting complete with a sign-in sheet, coffee urn, and a tin of Danish Butter Cookies. The organization was wrapping up their monthly meeting. The chairman was pleading for someone to please take over the outreach and fundraising committees. The secretary read a listing of upcoming events. Everyone seemed more than neighborly and hospitable. Some of the Daddies were older than he was. Some were even stouter. He was not sure he had stumbled into the right room. But as the meeting was adjourned all the metal folding chairs were screeched to the sides and stacked. Long folding tables were set up each with its own sub category of torture devises. He felt more than a little self-conscious being there alone. Not owning any leather except his vaguely corporate jacket, he'd put together an outfit of an old a plaid flannel shirt, denim vest, torn jeans and ox-blood Doc Martens. He was obviously an outsider but the harnessed and mustachioed members were amiable and beckoned him to each waiting table. There was the rope table, the cigar table, the electric shock table, the clips and clamps table, the mummification table, the whip table, and the mask and gag table. Each had one or two specialists to explain techniques and to hand out brochures. Everything, it turns out, was for sale.

He knew enough about cigars as torture from the 24-hour car rides to Mississippi he used to take with Uncle Hugh and his family each summer. The concept of electric shock as sex play was new to him. After two jolts from the display model "wand" he knew it would never be something he'd enjoy. The mummification presentation just seemed downright silly. Some naked fat queen wrapped in multi-colored saran wrap with nose and mouth tubes. The behind-the-table expert tried his best to convince him and the other onlookers of the sensual pleasure of being bound in plastic wrap but … dumb, it looked dumb.

As he table-hopped from "clips and clamps" to "masks and gags" he struck up a wordless eye-contact kinship with a much younger, much thinner, tattooed and pierced fellow solo window-shopper. This kid had put together a much trendier variation on the S&M aesthetic: shaved head, wire rim glasses, ancient blue and white The Smiths T-shirt, kilt over ripped jeans, and knee high lace up boots. Some of the more hardcore regulars regarded this upstart as an alien on their turf, while others clearly wanted to wrap him up, take him home and play Daddy to the wiry young punk.

The youngster gestured over to the whip table. That's where he first saw Master Lee. He and the kid were the only ones at the table. Master Lee began to explain the difference between cat-o'-nine-tails (nine tails) and floggers (more than nine) and the variations among the different leathers used. How each produced either more of a thwack or more of a thud. The thwack was a stinging sensation; the thud was one of pressure. The shinier the finish, the more of a thwack. Master Lee, with his Hun gray eyes, blond crew cut, and goatee encircled lips asked which he was into. Not sure, he thought for a moment. Since he definitely had *not* been into the sharp pain of the electric wand or the nipple clamps he said, "The thud I guess."

Master Lee picked up a beautiful sample. "Twenty-seven strands and all genuine moose-hide, want to try?" He admitted that he'd never done anything like this, but Master Lee reassured him. "Here, take off your shirt and come over to the wall."

That this crowd cared less about fitness fascism than most of New York made taking his shirt off in this room less intimidating than it would have been at the pool or the beach. What did give him pause was that, as often happened in

Manhattan, he was one of only a few colored folks present. In fact, he was the only Black man in the room. As his New Wave friend silently urged him on, he was super conscious that he was about to have his fat black back flogged in public by an Aryan-looking demi-god. "If they could see me now…"

The lashing itself was ordinary and intense. Black Southern Baptists had raised him, so the idea of the belt or switches was not new. Master Lee told him where to place his feet (just wider than shoulder width), where to put his hands against the wall, when to breathe. Breathing, it turned out, was important. It was how the two men communicated. The rhythm of the lashes increased in frequency and severity. Blood flowed to the surface, just beneath the skin. With Master Lee's calm steady voice talking him through it, he forgot that he was in a florescent-lit rec room with the smell of burning coffee. He had visions of *Roots*, or Mandingo, or that Haitian who had been tortured by cops in that Brooklyn precinct. The syllables, "At-ti-ca" escaped his lips with each timed exhale like a staccato mantra. There must have been around a hundred leather queens milling about. Some of them must have been watching this scene, but he was unaware of them until Master Lee said, "O.K. big guy, looks like you're enjoying this a little too much," and abruptly stopped. A line had indeed formed, each slave eagerly waiting his turn at the expert hands of the Master.

He sheepishly put on his flannel shirt, aware that there was a sizable swelling in the front of his pants. Master Lee smiled and handed him his business card. He worked out of Jersey, but made house calls as well. He thanked him and slithered

103

away. His silent young companion had vanished. Alone on his way home he fanaticized about taking the PATH train across the Hudson River for a little one-on-one, or of hiring Lee to come to his cluttered little apartment. He knew he'd never do either but that card was still buried somewhere in the "late 1980s—early 1990s strata" on his desk.

Suddenly he realized that well over an hour had passed and thinking about masturbation wasn't the same thing as doing the deed. "Nothing like cheating on yourself," he thought. There was a deep moist dent in the mattress where his dull mass had sunk. The day had slipped officially into mid-afternoon so he'd better get his fat ass out of bed. Now.

He pulled on something that passed for clothes, drank O.J. straight from the carton and sat down at his desk. It was a table really. Piled with the archaeology of the chaos and stasis of his life. Bills, cassettes, CDs, floppies. Coins, business cards, receipts, phone cards. Ashtray. Hand rolled bidis cigarettes from India. Old watch, old pens, Chapstick, empty breath mint boxes. Lots of dust. In the middle of this, his ancient and creaky laptop. We've almost made it to the end of the second millennium, now what?

His walls, not all of his walls but some of his walls, were covered with mottled black mold. It thrived in the heat and was probably giving him cancer or something. The air in his apartment was so fertile for slow-mo deterioration. It was the only place he felt at home. The phone machine worked. The mice had left him. He needed to leave himself. He trudged down the five flights to his mailbox. Junk mostly. And bills. And letters lying that he was "approved" for things he did not want. But there was also a yellow slip from his letter carrier telling him that this was his final notice of a package waiting for him at the post office. That's who had rung the doorbell.

He slogged through the hazy heat of an August Saturday to get the slip to the Post Office on time. They close early on Saturdays and he wanted to get his parcel. The building was frigid-aired. There was only one person in line ahead of him, he thought, "Good omen." The package was from his sister. He tore it open right there at the Post Office. A sweet thank you note from her and Dwayne for the terrific gift and a copy of the wedding on VHS videotape. He reproached himself for wondering if it included selected shots of the honeymoon night. Dwayne was a babe. Back in the haze he stopped by the Donut Shoppe for a bow tie and an iced coffee "light and sweet." He puffed up the five flights to his apartment, cleared away months of bills, *N.Y. Free Press*es, and Chinese take-out menus to create an area on the futon-on-a-frame big enough for him to sit on. He unwrapped the pastry and popped in the cassette.

What he saw horrified him. Floating amid the relatives and the strangers; the cake and the tulle; the tossed birdseed and the champagne toasts was this being who spoke with his voice and wore his clothes, and responded to his name. But this creature, this creature was huge. Humongous. Fat, fat, fat. He could not recognize this mass that cruised the hors d'oeuvres as having anything remotely to do with himself. Not even a distant and ostracized cousin. Certainly no friend of the family. How many pounds did they say the camera added? Not these many. It was bizarre. Like science fiction. Like, when did this happen and how did they do it to him without him noticing. The fiends. Diabolical aliens had invaded his body with massive injections of adipose. He hated them. On the tape, however, the whale is smiling. Arm proudly around his slender white-clad sister. Leading his svelte widowed mother out onto the dance floor. Lifting a teeny flower girl up over his head. Civilly chatting with his skinny ex-boyfriend who'd become a prominent lawyer and remained close to the family. The ex was there with his new lover, a short med student twelve years his junior. And 135 pounds if he was an ounce. And the creature's clothes. It wore the discontinued Armani jacket that he was still paying for three months later. In the three-way mirror in the remaindered section at Today's Man the jazzy oversized hound's tooth pattern had made him look hip, stylish, dashing, a bit rakish even. Swaddled around this grinning blimp at the buffet table it shouted corpulence. The rake swelled to avuncular. Debonair blew up to portly.

Stop! He pressed "STOP." He tried to regain some peace of mind by staring at the blue screen. He stared a long time. "Thanks, Sis." The large sugar glazed donut was becoming soggy in his sweaty palm. The ice in the coffee was melting, turning it watery tan. He took a bite, chewed, took another, chewed some more, sipped some sweet thin coffee through the straw. "Ah, the body functions are still operating," he thought.

He allowed his eyes to stray from the TV screen. He began to survey his apartment. It used to be so homey, artsy, "nice." It had degenerated into a repository of stale smells and heaps of crusty dishes, soiled clothes and junk mail. He felt entombed beneath paper and appliances that no longer worked. Newspapers and magazines lay mulching on his floor. Juicer, blender, crockpot were all blanketed under a layer of greasy dust. The leaky faucet in the tub trickled gallons from the city's reservoir everyday but he was too embarrassed to let the super in to fix it. Juan Carlos would be revolted by the chaos in which his fat body dwelled.

Once he'd filled out a questionnaire in one of the free bar magazines regarding sex practices. In response to the question "What is the one (sexual) thing you would never do for any amount of money?" he answered that it would have be anything to do with Scat. He was inordinately repulsed by shit. As a reality and as a concept. Which meant he had a fair amount of fascination for it as well. Smelling other people's shit was truly offensive to him. He would dry heave when he came across someone else's turds in a public toilet. Then how should we understand that his favorite pornography all featured liberal amounts of rimming? Of fisting? And butt fucking? Even as a little kid he always wondered stuff like—did the Queen of England take off her crown when she used the toilet? Did the Pope? And about the Invisible Man, besides being uneasy once he realized that the main character of the TV series must have been completely naked when he was doing his unseen antics amongst the townspeople, he also wondered this, as the man ate those apples in that cheesy 1950s special effect, when, exactly, would the apple, in actuality, become part of him and disappear? Was there a time after the apple'd been bitten that it should have become slowly vanishing mush as it mixed with invisible saliva? What if the Invisible Man took the bite, as he did in many episodes, then immediately spat it out, what would happen then? And when the Invisible Man pooped the apple, would the poop be invisible as well or would it reappear once it was no longer a part of the man? These thoughts like his endless inner debate as to who would win a battle between Jesus and Superman filled his childhood head. In reality, all these questions still troubled him. When reduced to an abstraction he could contend with shit. He could metaphorically hold it and study it like a peach in his hand. He could consider it, question it, concoct endless theories about it. But once that peach had been eaten, digested and shat out—even the discovery of his own turds found hours later, unflushed, floating, and leaching brown in his own toilet of his own apartment would send him reeling from the bathroom, his throat and abdomen constricted, nose scrunched into an angry knot. He'd have to reenter the room hesitantly and blindly grasp for the handle to flush without looking at the gorgon in the bowl.

And so it happened, about three weeks ago the Ukrainian lady who lived downstairs knocked on his door to tell him that whenever he flushed his toilet it was leaking into her bathroom and it smelled very bad. This information mostly was conveyed by hand and facial gestures that were absurdly decorous given the subject. Because he was too embarrassed to allow the super in to see his flat in its condition of moldering decay, he'd been trying to not use his toilet for the past three weeks. Peeing in diners or in bars was no problem, but pooping had become a real challenge. Because his preferred manner of defecating—squatting on the toilet rim—necessitated him getting undressed from the waist down, his routine of shitting only at home had been reinforced. But now, not being able to use his own toilet without offending his neighbor downstairs, it was necessary for him to piss into Chinese take-out soup containers and pour it carefully down the bathtub's drain and his new ritual for bowel movements was this:

1. Burn a stick of the overly sweet incense his ex and the B.F. brought back from their trip to India,

2. put down several sheets of newspaper,

3. squat and crap,

4. wipe with a dampened paper towel,

5. wrap the paper folding all four sides tightly,

6. put the contents into a plastic baggie,

7. place that bag into another plastic grocery bag, tie tightly,

8. finally, on his next outing, take the package five flights down to the neighboring building's trashcans.

Somehow this level of ritual allowed him to overcome the challenge. He thought, "I'm gonna have to clean this sty or leave."

On his way to the subway he passed that weekly farmers' market at Tompkins's Square Park. Country folk brought in their country fare to sell to those who were too poor or stupid or apathetic to escape the city's summer. The bins of the market were overflowing with some horrifyingly red tomatoes and other overpriced organic produce. He craved pizza. He walked across the street to Nino's and bought a slice with extra cheese. And a diet iced tea. He crossed back to walk through the market. He walked pass a mound of dog shit; someone had already stepped in it.

The subway station was thick with urine steam. He waited. He waited. He waited. He tried to hold his breath, and inhale as infrequently as possible. This didn't work because at the end of each airless interval he would then have to gulp a huge lungful of the nasty stuff just to keep living. He waited. When the train finally did come, the air conditioning was so strong that his sweat crystallized over the skin of his entire body. He could almost hear it tinkle. At first this felt good after swimming in the hot piss soup. Then the cold became painful. He wished he had a sweater, or his leather jacket. His joints ached. His nipples became erect and tender under his cold damp shirt. He welcomed each local stop when a brief breeze of warm foul air would waft in with the new passengers.

At 14th Street a couple sat across from him. At first they were totally unremarkable. Late 20s, Slavic, in tee shirts, shorts and healthy looking sandals. The guy was a good looking beefy blond with a thick neck and milky pale skin with flushed cheeks; she was ruddier and had dark brown hair with parted bangs and a long ponytail. She was slim and not unattractive. What became fascinating about them was how physically close they were sitting. The train was far from crowded. There was no real need for them to be sitting there so entwined. Their bare knees were touching; the fingers of her left hand were woven into his right; she lay her head on his shoulder and closed her eyes and dozed. He poked the flesh on her forearm to make a little white dot. Testing for burn. She opened her eyes; looked into his; smiled; went back to resting on him. Looking at them across the smelly subway car he thought, "I'll never have that."

"Or that." At 33rd a Black father and son came on board and sat next to the couple. The son was about twelve. He guessed that the father was a little older than the couple, but still was probably quite a bit younger than he was. They sat there like an affectionate illustration of genetics from a high school biology book. The angle of their heads, the alertness in their eyes, the way they both crossed their arms and left their legs parted open at exactly 45 degrees could have only been taught through chromosomes. "I'll never have that."

He had to get off. The train was too frosty and full of longings. 59th

Street. He'd go to the park. Uptown amid the manifestations of wealth, the heat felt more bearable. The grandeur of the ornate towers made him feel at peace with living in this city, even in sweltering August. There was a particularly magnificent gingerbread building just near the park. Outside there was a handful of people praying.

Then he remembered he had once left that same building through its bronze and glass doors. Newly arrived in the City, twenty-three and a half years ago he had exited the offices of the East Side Women's Center into the steely gray cold of a January sky. His arm encircled her to keep away the howl of winter and the brusque of midtown pedestrians. At the avenue he tried to hail them a taxi. They waited. They waited. Finally, a large toy-like Checker cab stopped. The driver's name was Chryshna. He lived in Queens. He drove like a fiend and talked without breathing. He had very definite opinions about race relations in the city. With both arms now around her, his nose buried into the wool of her scarf, he wanted to shout at Chryshna to shut up and drive more carefully, slowly. He also wanted to get her to her home quickly so he said nothing and smelled on her a combination of bubble gum, cigarettes and whatever they'd used to knock her out. He uncrumpled the single sheet of paper that had "After Care" printed at the top. He read the meager list. The driver screeched the cab at her street. He slid Chryshna a ten through the Plexiglas, not waiting for any change. "Thank you, thank you, friend." He wanted to carry her home, literally. She stopped, dug in her purse for some bills and said, "Get me some napkins and extra-strength Tylenol." "Napkins? Sure, sure. I'll get them," he said refusing her money. By the time he got to her place she was already lying on the futon on the floor, covered by a soiled comforter. A space heater radiated dusty warmth.

"You want a Tylenol?"

"Give me two."

"You want me to stay?"

"No."

"I'll call you tomorrow."

There was no response. He zipped up his down coat then remembered the check he'd made out earlier for his half. He started to say ... but just left it on her kitchen table under her Panda salt shaker, tiptoed out and quietly locked her door with his key. He thought, "Chryshna, now that's an interesting name for a boy."

He didn't know how long he'd been standing there sweating on the opposite sidewalk. Heat and humidity had robbed the spirit from the right-to-lifers. They listlessly handed out their fliers to the few passers-by who'd take them. Mostly they just walked in circles. Like a sudden attack of acid reflux, he had an impulse to scream at them and make them disappear. But the moment passed like a vaguely sour burp and he ... "What's the point," he strayed off into the park.

There was a "Spanish" family sitting next to the lake. He sat next to them on the rocks. There were generations there. History. He wanted to be included in their easy interactions. Scolding mom. Teasing brothers.

Annoyed older sister. Revered grandmother. He tried to disappear and yet be somehow linked with them. Every once and a while he would see one of the sons look at him, not quite hostile, but with an implied warning. He would then make some gesture like adjusting his sunglasses or checking his watch to say, "I'm not looking at you or your family." They'd leave him alone.

When he'd left her alone on her futon, in pain and sadder than he could imagine, he'd meant to go straight home to do whatever he did when other people might pray or cry. It's just that that bar was between her place and his. He stopped in for just one drink but found himself chatting up some French-Canadian tourist. He can't remember what they talked about. The tourist was cute in a hot sort of way. He came back home with him almost too easily. He fucked the tourist really hard. Twenty-three and a half years later that's what he can remember. That and that afterwards the French-Canadian burst into tears and sobbed, "Last night someone did something extremely violent to me." He felt that he should ask who or what but he didn't. He just held "Jean-Claude" whimpering in his arms until he was ready to dress and leave. Then he lay stinky alone in the dark imagining taking a young Chryshna to play soccer in the park.

In the park by the lake the Spanish family was loud. They blared Spanish music from a boom box, and spoke Spanglish noisily to each other. They drank secondary colored sodas from liter bottles and ate chicken from a large cooler. At some point two of the sons in their early teens began throwing empty plastic bottles into the lake. Like aristocrats viewing a regatta from a perfect shore, they watched the wind sail the plastic bottles away. Their grandmother was delighted by this and laughed and laughed. He was not delighted and did not laugh. He no longer wanted to be a secret member of this family. He wanted to wade into the water and gather those bottles and dump them ceremoniously into a recycling bin right in front of that littering clan. He could have been beaten up, or verbally challenged, or laughed at. He had to move on.

He headed north around the lake. He paused to buy a hot sausage with mustard and sauerkraut and onions. He bought a Diet Coke. He sat down on a bench and watched the rowers. At first the cinema-like lovers-in-the-park scene calmed him. But then their posturing irked him. Their "love" seemed so real, but how then could it be genuine and so picture perfect at the same time. Guys were rowing their ladies over mossy water. Splashes and giggles. Weeping willows trailed their branches. Lush greenery all around. Gothic Towers just beyond. Swans and ducks and the occasional heron dunked for fish or waterlogged bread. And everyone, lovers and waterfowl alike, seemed to be oblivious to the heat that was making him sweat onto the already mushy bun of his sausage. He finished it in three bites and gulped down his soda.

For years he thought the area of the park just north of the lake was called the "Brambles." He always called it that and no one ever corrected him. When he finally found out that it was in fact called the *Rambles* he wondered if for all those years, people had thought he was very clever, or very stupid or he just had a very weird speech impediment. No one ever corrected him. Not that he talked about the "Brambles" all that much or to just anyone. It was just that this was his favorite area of the Park and every trip up there would include a hike though its darkly wooded maze of large trees and hidden nooks…

"Bird watchers and cock suckers, that's all that's there," an old drunk at a bar once said to him when he mentioned that he'd spent an afternoon in the "Brambles." No one ever corrected him. "You ain't got no binoculars so I guess we know which one you are." Laughter all around. In fact, he'd never "sucked cock" in the "Brambles." The truth was he was much more like the bird watchers. Sure, he was drawn to the deep musky lure of male-in-male sex that exuded from those woods, but he'd never approach anyone there, and he was almost never approached. The few times older less in shape balding gentlemen or vaguely dangerous looking youths would come up to him, sit beside him, make eye contact with him, he would regard them with such contemptuous disdain that they would skulk off to their next object of prey. It was this ritualized mating dance he loved to observe. Like pigeons dragging their tails on the ground with ridiculously puffed out chests, these guys displayed and beckoned in a rite that was pure zoology. He could watch it for hours. And he did. Like a tracker he'd follow at a discrete distance, so as not to cause flight. His heart leapt when two would pause, pose, show their plumage. He'd dismay if they flew off in different directions, rejecting each other and denying him the opportunity to catch a glimpse of real faggots mating in their natural habitat. He'd have to choose which to follow, which to abandon. But if he were patient and quiet enough he almost always was rewarded with the spotting of actual fellatio in the field.

He spied two specimens on the brink of contact: a fifty-something year-old White fellow in topsiders, no socks, khaki shorts and a salmon colored Polo shirt; his companion, a twenty-five-ish dreadlocked Hispanic kid in a tangerine tank top, baggy jeans that came to mid-calf, and some brand-name sports shoes. The younger man was short, slender and flashed an air of treachery that could be seen even from far away. He'd seen this boy in the "Brambles" several times before. The first time he'd seen this boy he thought that it might be the cutest-dancer-with-the-dumbest-name from Blanche D's, the go-go/hustler bar he'd begun frequenting about two years ago.

Blanche D's was a relic. Part ghetto; part Weimer; part Columbus, Ohio Theater District. Even as other sleazy Times Square establishments were being shut down all around her, Blanche D's dyke owner had somehow been able to keep her business opened by paying off the right city officials and holding her dancers to the legal side of genuine nastiness. In the bar upstairs with its framed posters of long closed Broadway hits, White bartenders in white shirts, black vests and bow ties served waiting hustlers and their johns. The not-White dancers only worked the throngs of mostly colored, mostly beyond middle-aged gentlemen down in the darkened cellar. The combination of linoleum floor tiles, construction paper decorations, crepe paper streamers, shiny smiling brown faces and the smell of Black hair-care products reminded him of Baptist church receptions from his youth. He'd never seen the cutest-dancer-with-the-dumbest-name in daylight, but in the dim, mysterious atmosphere of the sweaty basement that young man was flawless.

However, the dreadlocked lad being fellated that day behind a stately elm in the "Brambles" wasn't the cutest-dancer-with-the-dumbest-name. Attractive, yes, in a semi-thug sort of way, but the stance, the angle of shoulders, the indifferent grip on the head of the khaki shorted papi were all too "street" to belong to the Blanche D's dancer. From his secluded bench in the "Brambles" he watched while the White gentleman with silver hair and a lobster tan nursed on the mocha sex of the wannabe gangsta Rasta. The wannabe gangsta Rasta gazed at a far off branch. At a woodpecker, or hummingbird perhaps.

One night last spring when he'd finally gotten up the courage to clumsily crumple a dollar into the bejeweled jockstrap of the cutest-dancer-with-the-dumbest-name the boy told him "I'm from the Bronx, but I'm Puerto Rican if that's what you 'aksing,' Playboy."

"Where are you from?" he'd asked, while squeezing the boy's little satiny hairless buns. The next month as his lips brushed the dancer's shoulder and he smelled marijuana in the dreads and coconut oil on the skin, the dancer told him of a Memorial Day spent taking acid with the family. As they gave each other Eskimo kisses the following week, he imagined a Puerto Rican edition of a Norman Rockwell Saturday Evening Post cover while the dancer told him of going fishing with "my Pops."

The next week after the dancer had turned around and started grinding bare butt into the front of his pants he whispered to the boy, "You're scary". The dancer answered smiling, tossing his dreadlocks and looking over his shoulder, "Yeah, but in a good way, right?" as he continued undulating while surveying the scene in a mirrored wall. The next night while he toyed with the ridge of the dancer's condom constrained cock head and pawed the naked, shaved ball sac the dancer told him one of his girlfriends might be pregnant. The cutest-dancer-with-the-dumbest-name wasn't ready to be a Daddy like some of the other guys working there.

"And just how old are you?" he asked the dancer mindlessly as he practiced minor scale finger exercises up and down either side of the boy's butt crack. When the answer was "twenty-three" he couldn't believe the words dribbling from his mouth when he then inquired, "Which sign are you?"

The youngster didn't seem to be bothered at all by this hackneyed request and replied as he rippled, "Scorpio, November 18." Doing the math he thought, "when I was his age the cutest-dancer-with-the-dumbest-name was a 4-month-old fetus!"

He knew the cutest dancer's dumb name because it was incorporated into a tattoo on his upper arm that was rendered in an overly ornate script. When, after months, he was finally able to decipher it during a lap dance his erection had melted like marshmallow fluff. He knew it was silly to be bothered by a person's name when the most meaningful relationship he'd been able to sustain for years involved this—him sliding, crinkling, stuffing currency into the under garments of this exquisite young man in exchange for three and half minutes of real feigned intimacy. He thought," We are soul mates," as he touched the rubber bands binding the dancer's genitalia into a petrified throb. This sent the dancer bolting back to the dressing room because, "I'm ready to 'pop'." And so what if he was the cutest-dancer-with-the-dumbest-name. If parents gave their babies names that would sound good being shrieked by lovers at the moment of orgasm we'd all be called "God," or "Shit," he mused.

Some nights after the dancer cashed in singles for twenties and left Blanche D's he'd follow the boy. Once or twice, well maybe three times, well, to be honest, on about a dozen occasions he shadowed the boy. One night the dancer and two others who were also Puerto Rican and exactly his height got into a waiting town-car. Twice he trailed after the three of them into one of the few remaining porn shops in Times Square where they bought bootleg kung fu videos. Usually he'd just watch them get a slice, or a falafel or a burger then take the Lex presumably up to the Bronx together. But one night, a couple of weeks ago, after a lot of furtive Spanish back-and-forth with the posse, the cutest-dancer-with-the-dumbest-name left Blanche D's all alone. He had to follow him.

The dancer didn't go buy Jet Li tapes; didn't stop for pizza; didn't head for the Lexington Avenue Line and the Bronx. Keeping half a block behind and on the opposite side of the street so as not to be seen, he tracked the dancer east to a classier neighborhood. The dancer rang the bell at a building that had only a few loft-like apartments. He watched as the dancer was buzzed in. He waited. He saw the dancer and someone else near the windows on the third floor. He'd been told that the cutest dancer had a side business selling weed; there'd been a three-month suspension from Blanche D's because of that last winter. He waited. He assumed the dancer was just making a delivery. He lit a cigarette and sat down in the doorway of a closed art gallery across the street. He looked at his watch. 2:47 A.M., this was dumb. O.K., he'd only wait 15 minutes or two cigarettes more. This was a quiet side street, but when the occasional after-bar couple would approach, he'd pretend to be a homeless man nodding off in the doorway. 3:26 A.M., this was beyond retarded. He was out of smokes and was nodding off for real. Finally, at 4:06 A.M. his heart stuttered when the lights on the third floor went off and the cutest-dancer-with-the-dumbest-name never left the building. Walking the 30-some blocks home it was almost daylight when he climbed into bed. Alone.

By the time the tangerine tank-topped boy and the salmon polo shirted papi had finished and parted it was late afternoon. The trees were casting long shadows eastward, but it was still oppressively muggy. At ease with his own lack of gratification, it was time to leave the Park. This time he headed to the West Side. Those avenues were crammed with adults younger than he was. Wealthier than he was. Cleaner and better groomed and of course thinner than he was. The heat didn't seem to affect them hardly at all. It gave them a gloss and sheen so that they appeared even more like magazine advertisements than they ordinarily would have. Tanned from their getaways to wherever, their perspiration looked as though it had been sprayed on from expensive imported spritz bottles. As he looked longingly at them eating their goat cheese and watercress with candied walnuts salads, sipping frosty tall iced cappuccinos or Pinot Grigios at sprawling outdoor cafes his own discomfort in this heat began to grow. His own crotch and pits were damp, but not in a shiny magazine cover way. He felt scratchy moisture in his ass crack. Tired throbbing behind his eyes, sweat beaded on his fat forehead. He could smell himself. His tongue worried with a strand of sauerkraut stuck in his teeth. He popped into an incongruously shabby deli and bought an over-priced ice cream bar. Out on the avenue he dodged a swarm of oncoming monster mommy strollers and plunged into the hot smelly hole to wait for a frigid train going downtown.

Waiting for a train to come and get him out of this seething fog of toxic odors, he was drawn to a tall rangy White man playing "Summertime" on sax in the middle of the nearly deserted platform. It felt so movie-like. It felt too right. He stopped behind a nearby pole to listen for a while. He thought about tossing some money into the guy's pitiful cardboard half box but the ice cream he was still finishing had cost more than two dollars and he knew that he only had two tens and a twenty and change. Getting nine singles for a ten from the box seemed somehow wrong and tossing in coins felt tacky. Humming "…fish are jumping, and the cotton is high. …" to himself, he moved further down the stinking platform. There was a model-pretty Black woman reading a tabloid standing too near the edge. The front page screamed another story about White cops being exonerated in the death of another Black male. He peered over her shoulder to see some more of the headlines and photos inside. The woman sensed him looking and she slowly pivoted toward him. He tried to make eye contact with her in a 1960s "right on sister" kind of way. She closed her paper and whisked herself over to where a few people were listening to the musician.

That headline had unnerved him. He tried to imagine his own confusion as the seventh of 19 bullets ripped into him, his wallet with his I.D. still in his black gunless hand. Or one minute he'd be hailing a taxi, the next he'd be hassled by cops posing as drug seekers, the next his life would be oozing out onto the avenue swirling among the spit and the blackened chewing gum. Or…

He could feel himself going a little bit crazy and maybe needing to give someone else a shove toward their after life. No, that wasn't what he needed. Did it mean anything that his greatest subway dread was not being pushed, or even pushing someone, but witnessing this act committed by others? Every time a train approached he'd cast around for any possible actors in this dramatic little fantasy.

Eventually the train did come and no one jumped or was pushed. In the refrigerated car he marveled that he wasn't living in the cartoon world of the Jetsons. His big fat ass was plopped on the cusp of the twenty-first century; wasn't his world supposed to be like the world of George Jetson now? But no, no flying cars, no moving sidewalks, no robotic maids. No ridiculous high collars and tight day-glow leggings. No "Jane his wife," no "daughter Judy." Just people being moved through a hole in the ground with sexier better-looking people pictured above them. The cute boys in the ads mostly had hair that looked as if it were wet but wasn't. Twenty-five years ago in another city on another train he used to stare in the morning at the wet hair of cute White boys and imagine them 15 minutes earlier, naked, getting out of their showers, toweling off with what would one day become the classic rock station blaring. A quarter of a century later the wet hair was fake. Hard as shale and it lasted all day. So that precise image of shiny wet hair with comb marks in it that would trigger a specific morning reverie of pale skin and deodorant and Steely Dan was now tainted by its presence during the afternoon rush. And commercial hair-care products had spoiled his memories of cute Black and Asian and Latin boys as well. In the ads above him, one national brand was marketing hair dyes specifically to this demographic. And the colors they were promoting were the exact off-shades that in his youth, fey black haired ethnic types would wind up with after adventures with bottles of peroxide. No "boy named Elroy."

He got off at the bottom of Manhattan. He'd take the ferry to Staten Island and back. It was free now, a pauper's cruise to nowhere. The trip over was uneventful. The breeze felt good. The gleaming and recently redone Statue of Liberty inspired what she was supposed to inspire he guessed. But he was always drawn to the other side of the boat. He loved the Verrazano Narrows Bridge. Like a slender piece of Danish Modern spanning the harbor.

While he waited for the return trip, he got a beer and a warm stale soft pretzel encrusted with salt. He squirted it with mustard. There was something about his childhood and hometown in doing that. Something about the Amish coming to market with their "thee" and their "thou" and their buggies and plain clothes. "We've always heard that Negroes sing so sweetly," an old Amish man had said to his den mother on one field trip to the market. "Could your boys sing us a song?" Eleven Negro boys, all at the brink of puberty serenaded the Amish family with a chorus and a verse of a very dissonant "Good Night Cub Scouts."

The ferry pulled away from Staten Island. He wandered out onto the forward deck. The bridge passed from sight. They were approaching The Statue as the cherry red sun plunked behind New Jersey. But standing out in the open on the way back he began to feel edgy. There was a tugboat pushing two barges directly in the path of the ferry. He was 99% sure they were going to collide with them. He swam badly. Were there any lifeboats on this thing? Any life vests? There was no collision. But then there was a swarthy man, really out of it, sitting on the floor of the deck being very loud, singing and crying to the songs coming out of his boom box. He was convinced the man was going to jump overboard. The man didn't jump. There were two bored Chasidic mothers who he thought weren't watching their seven kids closely enough as the children played close to the rail. He was very relieved when the ferry docked and he could step back onto Manhattan. It was finally night.

The southern tip of the island was a ghost town after dark. He didn't want to ride the subway again; he'd walk. He rarely came to this part of town. He took a right to the east. They say you can always get a cheap meal in Chinatown but he couldn't remember any specific restaurant or street names. He looked from sign to sign. The name of one street struck a chord. But it wasn't about food. It was about the postcard he'd been carrying in his back pocket for a week.

He reached into his pocket and pulled out the damp card. It was mostly milk chocolate brown with a line drawing caricature with big bulging eyes, corkscrew pasta hair, and a large oval mouth. A balloon bubbled from that mouth with the word "O-Tay!" printed inside. On the back side of the card was the info that a band was playing on such a date at such a time at KLUB KAOS. He squinted at the fading print; the day was today and the time was in about half an hour and he was just blocks from KAOS where he hadn't been for nearly ten years. After a couple of shrimp rolls and some mu-shu pork he would go check them out.

The band was his next door neighbors'. "Next door neighbors" was a genteel term for these beings. They were four scrawny skate boarders who lived in the apartment that mirrored his. Skater boy Travis' father Wade's undernourished girlfriend Kristin was the original tenant. When Wade and Kristin split up Wade stayed illegally behind. Then Wade moved out and let Travis move in. Travis had three of his friends join him to share the rent. All this is known because the boys wouldn't smoke in their tiny apartment and many summer late nights, early mornings, mid-afternoons their smoke and bits of their conversations floated into his bedroom from the fire escape they shared.

Although he could have lived without the smoke, he had become fond of their maddeningly inane al fresco tête-à-têtes. He imagined that their place reeked of old socks, beer and semen. Just picturing four nineteen to twenty-two-year-old straight skater boys living and sleeping together in a pint-size one bedroom apartment just a wall away made anything that came out of their mouths seem semi-deep. And sometimes, among the endless chatter about bands and movies and girls and boards there were such gems as—

"I don't especially like Alysa, but I need to do a virgin and she's just about the only one left."

Or—

"Dude, I'd never done anal before but she really wanted to, I mean I didn't have a condo and I'm not ready to be a dad yet, know what I mean. It felt O.K., but, dude, man, it was so fucking messy."

Or—

"Do you think Travis is gay? I mean it's O.K., I guess, if he is. It's just that him and, (name not understood), are spending a lot of time together. I mean a lot of time."

The only time he let them know that he was eavesdropping was once on a deliciously cool dawn when he was finally able to drift off and they woke him with their smoke and an eternally long debate about what to call their band. One kid, the lead singer he guessed, who looked mixed race in that New York City olive skinned boy with cornrows but who can really tell sort of way, wanted to call the band Buckwheat after the "Little Rascals" character. It was also one of his nicknames. Another kid came up with a name that was too insipid to be remembered now. Travis and the last boy wanted to call themselves Glass Grinder because that was "our sound" and "plus it's like we're making poison, you know grinding glass to put in stuff."

He needed to sleep. There was a breeze. A cigarette scented but cool lulling breeze wafting into his apartment after a week and a half of nights in the low-to-mid eighties and these dimwits were deep into this discussion that showed no sign of ever ending. Without thinking, without preparing, without knowing he would do it, he shouted out, "Why don't you just call yourselves The Buckwheat Glass Grinders and shut the hell up."

Ever since that morning, whenever they or their friends were out on the fire escape, Travis always made sure everyone stayed on their side and relatively quiet because "that old guy might be sleeping."

About five weeks after this he woke one afternoon to find the mocha colored card slipped under his door. On the back in an almost retarded scrawl was written, "Thanks for the name, Dude. Come see us." They'd dropped the "The" and the final "s" but he felt honored that he'd christened Buckwheat Glass Grinder. He put the card in his back pocket.

Nowadays on summer nights, when the lack of air and his own stench and bad thoughts would drive him from his apartment, he wound up in one of those Eastern European diners where he'd order cold borscht and egg creams and read the free weeklies until he was exhausted enough to return home and collapse. A decade ago he used to hang out late at clubs like KAOS, dancing alone amid the throngs, drinking beer after cheap beer until closing. That was before he began keeping count of his fellow revelers and calculating the number of those who were his age or older. One night when the club was packed with sweaty half naked bodies he could find only two guys and one grande dame who could even possibly be older than he was. But they were all thin as mop handles and had good hair. He decided that they looked pathetic pogoing among the embryos. And if they looked pathetic he and his unfashionable girth must look doubly wretched. He consigned KLUB KAOS to his past that very night.

After his Chinese food he got to the club about half an hour after the card said Buckwheat Glass Grinder would go on. Club time was usually an hour later than real time. Or at least it had been back in the day. But after being the only person *not* to be carded while waiting in a short line he caught only their last two songs. Buckwheat had his skinny braids bunched on the top of his head and stuffed into a knit cap. Regardless of the song, Buckwheat sang with his legs permanently apart and thrusting. Their keyboard player was a little rat-like boy who played with two fingers of one hand and paid a lot of attention to his postured smoking. Travis was on guitar and backing vocals. His complexion was so colorless it was translucent. Emotions, thoughts, whatever passed over his face like the clouds in those sped-up films from the 80s. Twitching from indifferent skater-dude to snarling rocker to slack-jawed weed-head to horny teenager all within two verses and a chorus.

The drummer was a cipher.

Their last song began as a cute folksy ballad. The intro sounded like a punk "Sounds of Silence:"

"I wanna do some smack,

Ooh, Ooh , Wadaya think about that,

Stoopid, I know you think Stoo-oo-pid.

But what do I care what you think,

I don't even care what I think, I think

I'm a canoe without any moorings

This god-fucking town is so bloody boring,

I hate all of my friends, I wish they'd just put an end to themselves

And to me as well.

I wanna do some smack, Whadaya think about that."

Then it devolved into faux heavy industrial Einsturzende Neubeuten cacophony. By the end even their friends weren't paying attention and were shouting conversations over the noise. There was no encore. He sat by himself at the bar and ordered a draft beer. He heard some other boys waiting to go on mistake him for an A&R man—one said, "Maybe he'll stick around and hear us," and the friend said, "Maybe we won't suck."

As Buckwheat Glass Grinder was breaking down he caught Travis' eye and gave him an ineffectual thumb up. Travis didn't seem to recognize him but nodded and continued hurriedly unplugging stuff. The band and a couple of fans hauled their instruments and cords behind a door covered with layers of ancient graffiti to what he remembered passed for backstage at KAOS.

On one sultry evening long before his self-imposed exile from KAOS, he'd found himself backstage drinking house red, smoking hashish, and shouting back and forth with a young woman who'd just played bass in band of girls called the Bitter Freuleins. He'd remembered seeing this girl and her drummer playing in Satan's Stepchild just before they broke up and the year before that they'd been together in Quizzical. The Freuleins had all the right make-up, clothes and hair. They had that School of Visual Arts attitude meets a bored European pose. Their morose and brooding sound had been a poppy drone just this side of ironic and sexy while skirting whiny and boring.

He'd thought the woman he'd been shouting with was very cute, which meant he'd thought she'd resembled a handsome boy. Her short black hair had been gelled into dangerous looking spikes; dark rings of kohl circled the lids of her light brown eyes. She'd had slender hips and almost no tits.

Red wine in places like KAOS was always a dubious choice; he had begun to get a nausea laced buzz-on and was having serious trouble following linear thought.

"My name is Mary-Josephine but they call me Garlic." Her words had swum to him through the throb of red wine and hashish and the next band's drum machine. It took a while for this sentence to paddle around in the swamp of his consciousness before he'd realized that it made no sense at all.

"What did you just say to me?" he slurred.

"Garlic, Gar-lic, Mary-Josephine, Gar-lic" she'd thrown the words out to him like lifelines. He'd continued to drown in his confusion. He took another dark drag on an enormous joint of tobacco mixed with hash she'd given him, coughed a bit, passed it back to her. All of a sudden it had surfaced through his mental miasma that she hadn't been speaking to him in English. In this noise and smoke filled club his drunken ears had been inadvertently translating Mary-Jo's sentence. She'd been shouting to him in Spanish; a lispy refined European Castilian Spanish. He must have said something to her in his drunken B-minus high school Spanish when they began speaking at the bar. When he'd told her he liked her band, perhaps. Or her hair. Anyway in Spanish she'd been saying, "Mi nombre es Maria-Josefina, pero me llamo Ajo." Then she'd emphasized the final "AH" sound from Maria and the initial "HO" sound from Josefina and said them together over and over, "Ah-Ho, Ah-Ho, AH-HO" Ajo, which is Spanish for "Garlic." Somewhere in the confusion of languages and chemicals he'd offered to carry Ajo's bass home to her near-by loft.

"Do you want me to do the Pony for you? The Pony for you?"

Fat

Ajo had been young. Way younger than he was. Biologically young enough to be his daughter he supposed. She'd posed at the foot of her bed that had been placed in the middle of an enormous yet somehow cluttered room in a Tribeca loft. Girl clothes had been everywhere. Feather boas, many pairs of high heels and combat boots, Catholic schoolgirl kilts, a corset on a mannequin. And odd objects like a stuffed iguana and a sealed jar in which floated the fetus of some mammal. A ceiling fan had swirled the air. Ajo had worn a plain white tank top and no panties. She had rinsed the gel out of her hair and it was wet with comb marks. She'd still had her lips and liner but had removed her lashes. His plump brown unclothed body had lain apathetic on her mattress wondering what her request meant in the larger significance of the universe.

"Do you want me to do the Pony for you? The Pony for you?"

He'd tried not to nod off. "Pony for you." He'd been drunk. Wasted. Maybe he'd needed to throw up some cheap red wine. She'd been earnest. Clean scrubbed in an earthy European way. He was amused through the ether of alcohol and whatever else he'd ingested. She was all young flesh and the stuff he thought he should want. "Pony for you." He'd wanted to want to fuck her. In reality he'd just wanted to go to sleep. Whatever music was playing was of the time. Not from the time of the Pony. Not from the future when he writes this. He'd been intrigued but not able to get it up. She hadn't seemed to care. And if she didn't care, neither did he. Come here, Child, and sit on my face. She'd obeyed without question. In truth he hadn't realized he'd spoken this command out loud. But he had. He used his

131

Yoga tongue exercises. She seemed to be pleased. It was "not without interest" probing up there among all the slick salty folds and stuff he was mostly unfamiliar with. She ground that stuff into his mouth. He gagged; suffocated. Needed oxygen. He pushed her up and gulped a mouthful of air. He lowered her onto him again. She was doing the Pony on his mouth. He imagined the next day. They'd interact, pleasantly but cool. She would make him coffee. After a quick shower it would feel positively gross to put on his smoke drenched clothes.

Suddenly she stopped her gyrations, brought her face uncomfortably close to his and said with a sort of a giggle, "O.K., Silly-Man let's fuck." He was not at all sure he liked this new nickname but he was sure he didn't have the will, desire, or stamina to pull off any sex act that required him to be awake. He rolled toward her. "Too tired, Ajo, in the morning, O.K.?" He tried to snuggle with her. She rolled away. He drew her toned and muscled back to his soft and plushy front. He stared at her hair, focusing on the skin and dandruff of her scalp. "If years ago we'd had the kid could it ever have grown up to be even remotely like this weird, puzzling gamine?" She smelled of patchouli. He fell asleep.

He woke up. It was the same night, the same bed with his same self and the same girl. But the gamine had transformed into a character usually played by chain-smoking, beautiful yet disheveled older European movie actresses. Ajo was rolling herself another hash and tobacco joint. "I want my sex, where is my sex?" This was not going to be easy. "In the morning, I promise. I'm wasted, you know, 'baracho'. Gotta sleep now, baby."

She shot daggers back at him. "Silly man." But he wasn't sure if she'd said that in English or … whatever. What he was sure of was that she wanted him out. Now.

This was going to be very easy after all.

"Hey dude, I thought that was you." Travis' voice snapped him out of the memory. He told Travis Buckwheat Glass Grinder had been awesome as he stared at the boy's thin white Guinea-T trying to determine if he was wearing nipple rings. The band and their friends were going off to some other bar he hadn't heard of but they didn't invite him to join them. He watched Travis leave, carrying his guitar case, his scruffy jeans several sizes too large for his gangly frame hung low down on his narrow hips exposing most of his plaid boxers. He had a watch tattooed on his left wrist, an angel's wing on each biceps and a bar code at the base of his skull; his wan face was pierced in many places; his dyed black hair gelled into dangerous spikes.

Now a female Japanese DJ was spinning French pop from the 50s, mixed with surfer riffs and a little Dionne Warwick. A scratchy vintage National Geographic film of bare breasted "native" women overlaid with slides of a high school science experiment were being projected as a background for the acts. He ordered another beer. He listened to two more middling bands. One in thrift store suits and ties played feedback so loud that it made his teeth chatter and his kidneys ache; the other looked like two college boys who'd just rolled out of bed and were checking their email in public by playing drips and drones on laptop computers. He ordered three more beers and a vodka tonic before the lights of KAOS were rudely switched on and it was way past time to stagger on home. "What's the name of that bar where 'The Wheats' were going? Can't remember."

It was sticky. It was tacky. The entire city smelled like boiling cauldrons of piss and fish and sugar. Shiny black garbage bags in front of high-priced restaurants were stirring with the squirms and squeals of scores of rats inside. He stamped his feet on the pavement in a little primal dance to keep the rodents out of sight. His toes curled inside his shoes. Air conditioners leaked warm droplets of other peoples' humidity onto his already moist skin on his long walk home; just as it had been so many years ago, when he'd staggered up from Ajo's Tribeca loft to his East Village tenement. Again he was racing the sun. He needed to be asleep before it rose and began simmering the seething stew of another day.

"They call me Garlic," he chuckled to himself. "Pony for you," he smirked. He hadn't thought of that girl and that night in such a long time. Years, actually. He crossed Houston. "Almost home to my womb of doom." He giggled again. Shit, when he was trashed and skanky he sure could crack himself up. No problemo. He was zigzagging his way over toward the lettered avenues. This was his favorite time of New York summers. It was so quiet, but still alive. There was that hum even in the calm. He stopped beneath an anemic dusty city tree because inside its dismal branches a choir of birds was singing as deafeningly and as gloriously as any heard in a Vermont forest. He had to imagine this, never having been in a Vermont forest. He stood there, immobile, listening as the eastern sky began to streak faint peaches and tangerines amid the lightening blues. "Over there is the east where Brooklyn and the Ocean and England are." He needed to piss. He hated adding to the city's stench but no way he was going to make the blocks to his building then up the five flights. He stood behind the sickly tree, and whipped it out. Just then a sports utility vehicle, or whatever they were called, screeched up beside him. A clean-cut White guy, in clean blue jeans and clean white running shoes got out of the passenger side. What was this? "Hey Bro, do you know where we can score some blow?"

He tried to finish his leak without getting his pants wet, but this was all so awkward. Didn't these bridge and tunnel junkies have any manners? He turned away from the young man as he tried to zip his fly.

"D'ya hear me, Bro? Hey whadaya got there?" This asshole had come over to the tree and put his hand on his shoulder. He's touching me. In that vulnerable space, caught, exposed, now being physically hassled, he reflexively spun and took a swing at the guy. It landed badly but caught the jerk off-guard and they both stumbled. He heard the driver's door open. He thought, "This can only get worse," and decided to give these suburban muggers his nearly empty wallet. "O.K., O.K., here," he reached into his back pocket. He wasn't sure if he heard, saw or felt it first. This made no sense. He was almost home. It was slowly becoming light. He needed to be in bed before it was bright. He definitely felt the second, third and fourth as he began falling to the ground. More heat than pain. No, that wasn't it. A painful singeing wet heat. He was down. There were two more. He could taste blood; he could see the gnarled roots of the pitiful tree. He felt his life oozing out onto the sidewalk swirling among the broken glass, spit and blackened chewing gum. From a thousand miles away he heard the words "no gun" and "back up" and "don't die." He heard sirens. He heard the distant thunder of angels drumming.

"Yo Bro, I said, do you know where we can score some blow?" his new "bro" called again from the passenger side. Jerked back to the here/

now he sneered, "Just keep driving east." The vehicle with its yahoos raced off.

All quiet. Even the birds stopped their chorus. He felt like he was in Chile or Indonesia or Rwanda or some other not safe place where he'd never been. He began walking faster.

Three minutes later he arrived at his building panting. He trudged up the five flights.

He was tired. He was just so tired. The sky was brightening on a new red-hot day. He peeled off his dank clothes, added them to the growing smelly mound on the floor. He buried his gross body beneath his dirty sheet. He burrowed himself into an unsettled sleep.

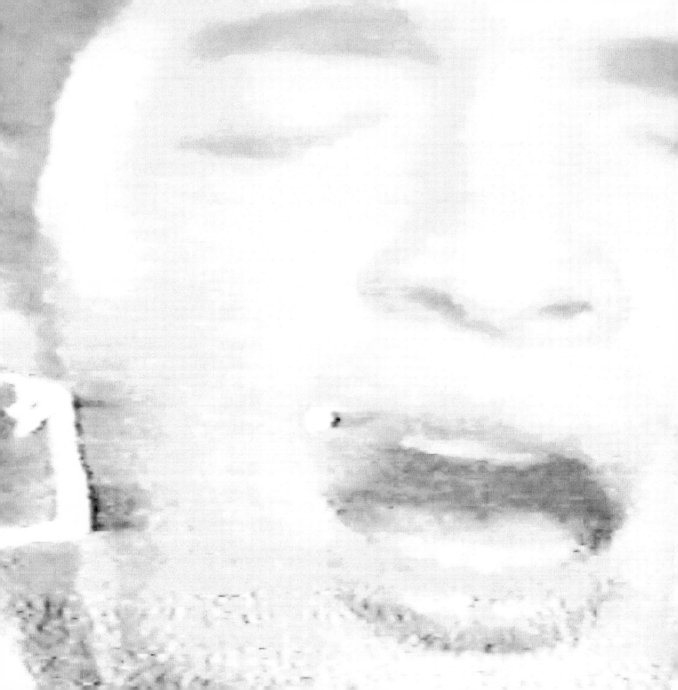

About These Stories

Certainly "autobiographical fiction" is not a creative strategy unique to me. It is probably what most, if not all, artists employ regardless of medium. If we are to "use what we know," what is it that we know better than ourselves? In translating our selves, whether it is through music, sculpture, writing or dance, we decide how to shape, highlight, distort, and mask who we are for a public to interpret. I consider all of the works in this collection to be autobiographical. At the same time, I know that they are all fictions as well.

I wrote *Prologue to the End of Everything* for a dance I created and performed at The Kitchen in New York in 1988. In the early 1980s I had traveled to Nicaragua to teach at the Universidad de Centro America in Managua and in villages in the countryside. This was during the war between the Sandinista government and the US-backed Contras;

some of my dance students were also Sandinista soldiers. Back here in New York several of my friends, lovers and colleagues had contracted a mysterious, new and often deadly disease. Those two realities triggered that writing and that dance.

I had moved to New York from Philadelphia at the end of 1979. Shortly after that I met the writer Dennis Cooper who had recently relocated from Los Angeles. I described our meeting in a 2010 interview in *ArtForum*:

> "When I first met Dennis Cooper he was reading at some club on the Westside. There was a buzz about him before his arrival in New York; people were really excited. I didn't know him at all ... When I heard him read, I was shocked that literature could upset me so much. It was something from *Tenderness of the Wolves*. And after I said, "Do you want to work with me?" And he said, "Sure," even though he didn't know who I was."

Dennis introduced me to work of young, mostly queer, experimental writers as well as to the work French porn director Jean-Daniel Cadinot. As we lived through the 1980s and 90s, the confusion caused by the specter of AIDS and its entwining of sex and death led my art into a darker Eros. The first dance-theater collaboration Dennis and I made, *THEM*, was reviewed by Burt Supree in the *Village Voice* – "*Them* isn't a piece about AIDS, but AIDS constricts its view and casts a considerable pall." In my own writing here, in both *Kim* and *Sebastian Comes for Tea*, there is sex but no one seems to be very ecstatic about it.

During this time, I felt that when writing about sex, many writers, myself definitely included, relied too heavily upon certain Erotic Lit clichés. I decided, based upon how my visual artist friends employed life models to hone their skills, I would place the following ad on America On-Line:

> "Gay writer / 40's, iso men to pose and to be interviewed. ALL types. Not necessarily erotic. And not looking for a "sexual" encounter. Just perverse research. Nudity. But minimal physical contact. Downtown Manhattan. +/- 2 hour sessions. Can be worth both our whiles."

This was the genesis of *Specimen 1*, *Specimen 2*, and *Specimen 3* written over the course of several years. By 2001, I was soliciting models in clubs, as in the case of *Specimen 4* and *Specimen 4a*.

Finally, *Fat*. I have been writing this one-day-in-the-life of an unnamed protagonist for almost two decades. Economics, race, sexual trial and error paint a picture of this unmoored and cumbersome soul, and of Downtown New York City on the cusp of a new century. As the man reflects in 1999, "We've almost made it to the end of the second millennium, now what?" It is important to remember: I consider all of the works in this collection to be autobiographical ... they are all fictions as well.

Ishmael Houston-Jones
New York, June 2018

Ishmael Houston-Jones is choreographer, author, performer, teacher, and curator. His improvised dance and text work has been performed in New York, across the US, and in Europe, Canada, Australia, and Latin America. Drawn to collaboration as a way to move beyond boundaries and the known, Houston-Jones celebrates the political aspect of cooperation. He and Fred Holland shared a New York Dance and Performance "Bessie" Award for *Cowboys, Dreams and Ladders*, which reintroduced the erased narrative of the Black cowboy back into the mythology of the American West. He was awarded his second "Bessie" Award for the 2010 revival of *THEM*, his 1985/86 collaboration with writer Dennis Cooper and composer Chris Cochrane. In 2017 he received a third "Bessie" for *Variations on Themes from Lost and Found: Scenes from a Life and other Works by John Bernd*. Houston-Jones curated *Platform 2012: Parallels* which focused on choreographers from the African diaspora and postmodernism and co-curated with Will Rawls *Platform 2016: Lost & Found, Dance, New York, HIV/AIDS, Then and Now*. He has received a 2016 Herb Alpert, a 2015 Doris Duke Impact and a 2013 Foundation for Contemporary Arts Artists Awards.

Houston-Jones' essays, fiction, interviews, and performance texts have been anthologized in the books: *Dance–Documents of Contemporary Art* (Whitechapel Gallery and MIT Press, 2012); *Writers Who Love Too Much- new narrative 1977 – 1997* (Nightboat Books, 2017); *Conversations on Art and Performance* (Johns Hopkins, 1999); *Footnotes: Six Choreographers Inscribe the Page* (G+B Arts, 1998); *Caught in the Act: A Look at Contemporary Multi-Media Performance* (Aperture, 1996); *Aroused, A Collection of Erotic Writing* (Thunder's Mouth Press, 2001); *Best Gay Erotica 2000* (Cleis Press, 2000); *Best American Gay Fiction, volume 2* (Little Brown, 1997); and *Out of Character: Rants, Raves and Monologues from Today's Top Performance Artists* (Bantam, 1996).

His work has also been published in the magazines: *Farm*; *PAJ*; *Movement Research Performance Journal*; *Contact Quarterly*; *Porn Free* and others.